Praise for Mari Carr & Jayne Rylon's
Western Ties

"All I can say is WOW! This book had me grinning from ear to ear and crying at the same time... An absolute must read!"
~ *Guilty Pleasures Book Reviews*

"*Western Ties* is the final book in Mari Carr and Jayne Rylon's Compass Brothers books, and it's a most emotional and yet supremely satisfying conclusion to this family epic. It's filled with passion, family devotion, disappointment, tragedy, and the feeling of coming home."
~ *Long and Short Reviews*

"A good read and a series you don't want to miss."
~ *Night Owl Reviews*

Look for these titles by
Mari Carr

Now Available:

Just Because
Because of You
Because You Love Me
Because It's True

Black & White
Erotic Research
Tequila Truth
Rough Cut
Happy Hour
Power Play
Slam Dunk

Second Chances
Fix You

Compass Brothers
(written with Jayne Rylon)
Northern Exposure
Southern Comfort
Eastern Ambitions
Western Ties

Compass Girls
Winter's Thaw

Print Collections
Learning Curves
Dangerous Curves
Love's Compass

Look for these titles by
Jayne Rylon

Now Available:

Nice and Naughty
Where There's Smoke

Men In Blue
Night is Darkest
Razor's Edge
Mistress's Master

Powertools
Kate's Crew
Morgan's Surprise
Kayla's Gifts
Devon's Pair
Nailed to the Wall
Hammer It Home

Play Doctor
Dream Machine
Healing Touch

Compass Brothers
(Written with Mari Carr)
Northern Exposure
Southern Comfort
Eastern Ambitions
Western Ties

Compass Girls
Winter's Thaw

Print Collections
Three's Company
Love's Compass
Powertools

Western Ties

Mari Carr & Jayne Rylon

Virginia,

So great to finally
meet you!

Jayne
Rylon

SAMHAIN
PUBLISHING

Samhain Publishing, Ltd.
11821 Mason Montgomery Road, 4B
Cincinnati, OH 45249
www.samhainpublishing.com

Western Ties
Copyright © 2013 by Mari Carr & Jayne Rylon
Print ISBN: 978-1-61921-112-4
Digital ISBN: 978-1-60928-566-1

Cover by Valerie Tibbs

First Samhain Publishing, Ltd. electronic publication: March 2012
First Samhain Publishing, Ltd. print publication: February 2013

Dedication

This book is dedicated to our parents for their Vicky-style love, their JD-like words of wisdom and their unconditional support and acceptance of our tendency to write *really* dirty books.

Prologue

Sawyer Compton waved goodbye to his father, JD. The taillights of the ranch's pickup dwindled as his old man drove away from the airport. Sawyer slung his bag over his shoulder more securely, wincing at the pressure the weight put on his too-new tattoo. His back was killing him. He wished he and Sam had managed to find time to get the tattoos right after high school graduation. Instead, the two months between pomp and circumstance and packing their duffels had been filled with chores on the ranch, travel plans, a huge going-away party thrown by their mom and the million other little things needed to pave the way to their future adventures.

As a result, they'd gotten the tattoos yesterday after Sam had stormed into Sawyer's bedroom as he stuffed photos of his brothers into the scuffed boots he'd never wear in basic but couldn't bear to leave behind. His twin, Sam, had snapped at him, saying, "Get your ass in the truck." He hadn't needed to be told twice.

Sawyer had wanted the tattoo since he was fifteen and seen the ink his oldest brother, Silas, had made a permanent part of his body. Since then, it had become a tradition for each of the Compton brothers to get the compass tat on their back, a symbol representing their coming of age and a tie to home as they explored their freedom. However, unlike Silas's, Sawyer's navigational brand wasn't pointing to the north. Rather he hoped it would eventually lead him west...to the Pacific Ocean, sunshine and—God willing—a shitload of California girls.

"Guess that's that." Sam turned and entered the terminal.

"Yeah." Sawyer followed Sam through the automatic doors. They'd scheduled their flights at about the same time, neither of them wanting to be the last brother at home with Vicky. "Gotta admit we were lucky JD talked Mom into staying behind or we'd still be standing on that curb out there."

Sam grinned ruefully. "No shit. As it was, I thought she might crack a few ribs during that never-ending goodbye at home."

Sawyer nodded. "My back is on fucking fire."

Neither of them had told their parents about their clandestine rendezvous with Snake, the ranch's unofficial artist. So Sawyer had gritted his teeth throughout his mother's bear hug, Vicky unknowingly hurting him. A part of him felt that pain was poetic justice. His parents were suffering with his and Sam's departures. His folks had four sons, and Sawyer suspected both JD and Vicky had been confident at least one of their offspring would remain close to home working the Wyoming land that had been in their family for several generations. Instead, all four Compton brothers had decided to seek their fortunes elsewhere.

Sam checked his watch. "Looks like we made good time. What do you say we check our bags and then hit the bar until takeoff time?"

Sawyer laughed. "We're eighteen, Mr. Hot Shit. They're not going to serve us."

Sam shrugged. "I bet I can charm us into a couple of microbrews. Especially if the bartender is a college girl."

Sawyer stuck out his tongue in the universal sign for *gross*. "Make mine a Miller Lite." He studied his brother's sweet Columbia hoodie, which Sam had picked up during orientation, and tried to forget how much he'd missed the fucker in the four days they'd been apart. "Besides, who's gonna be smart enough to hit the books at some fancy school but dumb enough to forget to card your scrawny ass?"

"Really, Sawyer? How many times have I explained why insulting your twin is ridiculous?" Sam laughed as he shook his head.

"Hey, not my fault you've spent all your time studying instead of working out in the barn."

"Are you referring to bucking hay or *bucking* Beth when her dad was roping the herd with JD?"

"Take your pick." Sawyer rubbed his flat belly and sighed. "We may have started out identical. Now I can kick your ass."

"Maybe if you were smart enough to catch me, baby brother. I still say we should have taken Snake up on his offer to make us identification."

"How are you gonna survive without me? Those fake IDs of his look like shit. We'd have been busted the first time we tried to use them, and JD would have kicked our asses."

"Fine, chicken. I won't tell if you indulge in one last watermelon fizz." Sam ambled toward the ticket counter.

Sawyer tried to ignore the lump clogging his throat. Saying goodbye to his parents had been tough, but leaving Sam and all the special things they'd shared—like his favorite drink—was going to be brutal. Despite their identical looks, their personalities were in direct contrast to each other, a combination that had pretty much guaranteed a lot of black eyes and split lips throughout their childhood. However, after Silas and Seth had left home, the younger Comptons found more common ground. In the past two years, Sam had become Sawyer's best friend.

They dropped their luggage off at the baggage check and made their way through security. Claiming a couple of stools at the bar, they ordered sodas. For several minutes, they sat in silence, watching people rush past—everyone dashing to catch flights somewhere else or taxis home.

Sawyer had suffered from that same impatience for years, desperate to leave Compton Pass, to forge his own destiny. Now, he was anxious to slow things down, and he couldn't help but wonder why in the hell he'd been in such a damn hurry.

"At least we'll be on the same coast for a bit." Sawyer played with the condensation on his glass. "Cape May's not all that far from New York City."

"You'll be in basic training for eight weeks. And then the Coast Guard will station you God knows where. Doesn't matter how damn close the cities are, it's not like we're going to be hanging out together."

"Yeah, but I get ten days off after basic. I'll come check out your fine preppy institution in New York before I ship off."

"More like you'd like to raid the coed dorms before you're forced to spend months in barracks with a bunch of dudes."

"Yeah well, I've waited a long time to use the I'm-leaving-in-the-morning, give-me-something-to-remember line."

"You've watched *Band of Brothers* one too many times, Saw."

He couldn't help it if the series had captivated him for more reasons than one. The military would help him reclaim what he'd lost when Silas and then Seth had abandoned the ranch. "Whatever. It'd be cool to see the Statue of Liberty."

"I'll take you around the city. We'll hit the clubs, and I'll show you all the fun we've been missing in Bumfuck."

Sawyer chuckled. Sam had always argued the grass was greener in the big city, while JD pointed out nothing grew in the concrete landscape where Sam was headed. Of course when

Sawyer considered his own destiny, he realized there wasn't much pasture to be found in the sand either. "I can't wait. Look, Sam..."

"Last call for passenger Compton." A shrill crackle blasted through the elevator music in the airport lounge. "Please proceed to gate 5A. This will serve as the final boarding call for flight 328 to Atlantic City."

"What the—" Sawyer bolted to his feet, digging in his Levi's for his boarding pass.

Sam saved the chair Sawyer had occupied from crashing to the floor. "I thought your plane left at three thirty."

"Shit!" He double-checked the info. "That must have been the flight number. It's scheduled for three o'clock."

"You better run." Sam shoved Sawyer toward the door. "It's already five after."

"But..." He wasn't ready. He hadn't even bumped Sam's fist or tugged his twin into a one-armed hug.

"Go!" Sam shooed him even as he turned to the waitress. Instead of asking for the check, Sawyer overheard his brother asking the pretty blonde if she could call the airline and tell them Sawyer was on his way. He even spelled their last name.

For a fleeting moment Sawyer wondered if it would be the end of the world to miss his flight.

"What are you waiting for?" Sam waved his arms like an agitated old lady.

"I don't know." He swallowed hard, his feet frozen to the ground. "You'll email, right?"

"Promise. Every day. I'll write you so many letters I'll put Lucy to shame." Sam's broad smile melted Sawyer's paralyzing terror. "How else will I make you jealous over all the ladies on campus?"

He didn't have the chance to worry about whether or not Sam's semesters would line up with his shore leave or when they'd make it home next. Like JD always said, "If you start a journey looking for the way back, maybe you're headed in the wrong direction."

Screw doubt. This was the future they'd spent most of their lives running toward. What sounded like paradise to Sam would be hell for Sawyer—almost as bad as staying here in Wyoming. He closed his eyes and imagined the sound of an ocean he'd only ever seen on TV. Anxiety drained away.

"They're waiting for you, cowboy." The waitress flashed a bright-white smile. She pointed. "Head that way, to the very end of the concourse. They said they'll give you five and then you're out of luck. You look like you'll make it."

"You *will* make it." Sam nodded as Sawyer stumbled out of the bar, picking up speed.

"So will you." He grinned over his shoulder before sprinting down the hall. He imagined Sam rolling his eyes at his lack of decorum when he bellowed, "Compass brothers rule!"

Chapter One

Seven years later

"Stop worrying, Stacey. I'm a big girl and I know what I'm doing." Leah Hollister looked around the crowded room. A shiver of anticipation, laced with equal parts of excitement and nervousness, raced up her spine.

Her best friend, Stacey, glanced toward the door for the thousandth time since they arrived at the private play party. They had been college roommates at the University of Wyoming. After graduation, Leah had gone home to Compton Pass to teach twenty-four unruly kindergartners, while Stacey was using her education degree at a high school in Los Angeles.

"Bill will be here soon," Leah tried to calm her anxious friend down. "He's the one who suggested we come early, remember? He wouldn't send us into a dangerous situation. These people are his friends."

A few months ago, Stacey had called to say she'd fallen in love. Leah had been shocked to learn that Stacey's new boyfriend was also a Dom who'd introduced her girlfriend to his lifestyle. Since then, Leah hadn't been able to stop thinking about the sexually charged stories Stacey had told her. To say her own sex life was lackluster was an understatement. It would be more accurate to say it was non-existent.

Stacey nodded. "I know we're safe, but I'd feel better if he was here to make sure you, I mean, we don't break some rule of the house or something."

Leah laughed loudly. "You had it right the first time. You

think I'm going to fuck this up."

Stacey sighed. "Are you sure you want to do this?"

Leah rolled her eyes. "Oh my God. We're not really going to have this conversation *again*, are we?"

"I want to know that you're going to take this seriously. These parties aren't games, Leah. They aren't jokes. The host has rules that he expects us to follow."

Leah observed the partygoers as Stacey spoke. She knew exactly what was expected of her. It was the reason she'd come to California, though she'd never admit that desire to Stacey.

"I know what's expected of me, Stace. You don't have to worry."

Stacey studied Leah's bracelet and shook her head. "Well, I have to admit, of all our friends at college, you were the last one I expected to bring to a place like this. Don't get me wrong, but you're sort of a goody-goody."

"Goody-goody? Shit, that's not a compliment. Why on earth do you think that?"

"You're straight as an arrow. I've never once seen you step a little toe out of line or take a walk on the wild side. In college, while we were all partying it up at the frat houses, you were in the dorm, doing homework."

"I was there on a scholarship, Stacey. I couldn't let my grades slide or I would have lost it."

Stacey nodded. "I know that. It's more than just the constant studying though. You are the queen of play it safe."

Leah gave her friend a frustrated sigh. "Did you ever stop to think that sometimes it sucks to be the reliable one, the boring friend, the designated driver for every single party? I want to cut loose, Stacey. I want to have my night."

Stacey's face radiated guilt. "You never seemed to mind

picking me up at the bars in college."

"I didn't. Not really. You were having fun. I'm pretty sure you got as much, if not more, out of your university experience than I did. Lately, I've been feeling restless. I don't know how to explain it. There's got to be more to life than work and shitty sex with losers."

Stacey's gaze traveled over her outfit. "Yeah, well, looking like you do tonight, I'd say it's a sure bet you're going to get a hell of a lot more. Never thought I'd see the day where you'd walk into a party dressed like that."

Leah laughed. "What? You don't see me as a sweet little submissive girl?"

Stacey snorted. "You're sweet, Leah, but I'm worried you may be a little *too* sweet for the kind of stuff that goes on at these parties."

Leah appreciated her friend's concern, but it was misplaced. She'd never felt more certain about any decision. She needed to try this or she'd spend a lifetime always wondering. "I'll be fine. I'll mingle and make conversation with the big bad Doms. See if I can entice any of them into huffing and puffing and blowing my house down."

"God. See? This is what I'm talking about. Ever since I picked you up at the airport, it's been one lame joke after another about this lifestyle."

Leah shrugged. "I can't help it. When I'm nervous, I make jokes."

"I wish Bill was here. If you speak to any of these men like you talk to—"

"Leah?" a familiar male voice behind her said.

Leah closed her eyes and prayed she'd imagined it. There was no way. No possible way—

"Leah Hollister?"

She sighed. Fuck. What were the chances?

Turning, she realized her night wasn't going to end as she'd planned. She should have saved her money. Should have stayed in Compton Pass. She was screwed.

"Sawyer." She didn't bother with the pretense of being happy to see him. "What the hell are you doing here?"

"Leah," Stacey whispered, her voice full of warning.

Sawyer narrowed his eyes, refusing to answer. His gaze started at the top, taking in her dramatic makeup, before drifting lower to her breasts, accentuated by the tight corset Stacey had loaned her. She willed herself to remain still as he finished his visual tour with a long look at her short leather skirt and stocking-clad legs.

"Enjoying the view?" she taunted. "You still haven't answered my question. Shouldn't you be in San Francisco? What are you doing here?"

He scowled. "That's my question for you. A BDSM party in L.A. is a long way from a kindergarten classroom in Compton Pass. Last time I saw you, you were leading a pack of five-year-olds around my family's ranch."

A couple of years earlier, Sawyer had helped her organize a field trip to Compass ranch. It had been one of the highlights of the year for her students—and for her. It was also the last time she'd seen Sawyer. Two years was a long time. She certainly hadn't expected their reunion to take place in L.A.

She sucked in a deep breath and tried to hide her disappointment. He was right. She'd purposely put herself as far away from home as possible, so that she could indulge in these two nights. One weekend to confirm a few suspicions she'd always held in regard to her sexual preferences. Sawyer was going to put a wrench in the works.

She gestured at her outfit. "I would think my role here is obvious." For the first time, she allowed her gaze to travel over him as well. Her body heated with arousal as she noted how unbelievably sexy he was. He wore tight dark jeans and a black T-shirt that hugged his muscular chest to perfection. No one in the place would fail to read the dominance in his stance, the aura of power he projected.

On the surface, she was shocked to find her friend in a place like this, but there was another part—deep inside—that wasn't a bit surprised. He belonged here.

"So you're a Dom?" She fought the urge to laugh as she asked the absurd question. Of course he was.

His gaze drifted to her arm. He grasped her wrist, pulling it up and toying with the white wristband the host had given her upon arrival.

"You understand what this means, right?" he asked, gesturing to the bracelet.

Sawyer completely ignored her Dom question. It didn't matter anyway. It had clearly been rhetorical. He was a Compton. Anybody and everybody from their neck of the woods knew that name was synonymous with alpha male.

She gave him an annoyed look. "Of course I do."

It was evident from his tone he didn't think she belonged here any more than Stacey. One of the reasons she'd planned this adventure far away from home, surrounded by strangers who didn't know her, was because rumors spread like wildfire in their small hometown. She knew about Sawyer's sexual proclivities, and she'd always wondered if she shared a few of them.

Besides, her *sweet* disposition didn't inspire the more adventurous cowboys back home to ask her out, so her opportunities for exploration were seriously limited. Stacey was right. She *was* a goody-goody.

Sawyer didn't appear to like her answer, so he restated the obvious. "It means you are an unattached submissive who's looking for a Dom. This wristband has declared it open season on you."

She shrugged, unconcerned. "Sorry to shatter the illusion, Sawyer, but I think I can handle whatever this party dishes out. It's not like I'm a virgin."

He frowned. "You lost your virginity in the backseat of a Pontiac to Les Prescott after Compton Pass won the district football championship our senior year. The guy was a shithead. You should've chosen better."

Leah laughed, though a ripple of desire slammed into her. It was always this way with Sawyer. Though they were just friends, there'd never been a time when she hadn't felt his gaze on her. He'd scared off more than a few would-be boyfriends in her lifetime claiming they were *only after one thing*. Les had fallen into that category, but Sawyer had been playing on that championship team and had been a bit distracted that night.

Sawyer had appointed himself her personal guardian in third grade when Jordan Haskiell had shoved her down on the playground after she'd beat him in a footrace. As a result, Sawyer had endured an afternoon in the principal's office and God only knew what kind of punishment at home after issuing Jordan a very physical, very painful warning of what happened to guys who messed with Leah. While Sawyer hadn't pursued her romantically, he'd certainly taken the bonds of friendship to a new extreme.

Despite the fact they'd existed in different cliques at school, Sawyer hadn't let social status stop him from being one of her best friends. He'd run with the jocks and cheerleaders, while she'd been firmly encamped with the brainiacs, less affectionately referred to as nerds by their peers. "How could you have known about Les?"

"I told you. He was a prick. He was bragging about it at school the following Monday."

She flushed. She'd never heard of Les spreading rumors about her. "I didn't know—"

Sawyer grinned. "Luckily, he started his boasting with me. I took him out behind the school and gave him a reason to shut his fucking mouth."

His admission held a hint of humor, but she could tell he was angry. She decided to test the waters to see how screwed she was.

"Well, it was great to see you again, but Stacey and I were going to pop over to the bar for a drink."

"I'll go with you." He confirmed her fear.

She smiled and shook her head. "No, I don't think that's a good idea. You're scaring off all the other Doms."

His wolfish grin let her know that was his intent.

Her temper sparked. "God dammit, Sawyer. Go away."

Stacey lightly touched her arm, alerting Leah that she'd spoken too loudly. Several people glanced in her direction and frowned. She was never going to achieve her goal at this rate.

Sawyer was the only person in the room who didn't take offense at her faux pas. "You realize this is a weekend party?"

She nodded. It was starting to look like it would be a long two days.

Sawyer reclaimed her hand, slipping off the white bracelet.

"What the hell are you doing?" She tried to pull her arm free, attempting to grab the wristband back.

Sawyer's grip was implacable. He reached into his pocket

and pulled out a green bracelet. Suddenly, she felt dizzy. There was no way he would—

Sawyer slipped it around her wrist.

"No," she whispered when he lifted her hand.

Sawyer leaned closer, his breath hot against her cheek as he murmured in her ear. "The host is going to come over to confirm you've been claimed by me. You're going to tell him you've agreed to be my sub. If you don't, I will personally drag you out of here, take you to the airport and load you on the first plane to Wyoming myself. Don't test me on this, Leah, because I promise you won't like the end result."

The host, Ronald Grey, was a large, attractive black man in his fifties who, according to Stacey, had more money than God.

Ronald patted Sawyer on the shoulder in a familiar, friendly manner and Leah wondered how in the hell a cowboy from Bumfuck knew such a powerful man. "You don't waste any time, Compton. You realize the green band signifies you're claiming this young lady for the entire weekend? A lot of the players are opting for the purple bracelet—a one-night affair— so they can sample another variety tomorrow night."

Leah narrowed her eyes at Grey's condescending comment, talking about her like she was a fucking dessert while warning Sawyer against gorging on one flavor. Sawyer squeezed the hand he'd never released, warning her to remain silent.

"When I see something I like, I take it."

Grey nodded approvingly before looking at her. "You consent for this man to serve as your Dom?"

Stacey had assured her that while the BDSM play was serious, no one would be allowed to touch her without her agreement.

Leah looked at Sawyer. Her plans were shot. He would do

exactly as he threatened. She nodded.

Grey collected the white wristband she'd received at the beginning of the night and looked at Sawyer. "You and your sub may participate in the public games or you can take her straight up to the room you were assigned upon arrival."

Sawyer thanked Grey and they watched the man walk over to another couple.

Leah stared at Sawyer, letting her annoyance show. He'd fucked up everything, and she wasn't going to let him off easy.

Stacey shook her head in amazement. "Wow. That was fast. I was worried you wouldn't meet anyone. Oh." Stacey gestured toward the door. "Bill's here."

Her friend looked to Sawyer as if seeking permission for something. Sawyer nodded and Stacey smiled, going to meet her lover.

"What was that?" Leah asked.

Sawyer's gaze hardened. "Did your friend give you any instructions about what your role would be?"

She nodded. "She told me a few things."

"And did you listen to her?"

Leah blew out a furious breath. How dare he act like this? He was the one who'd ruined her trip. "Listen, Sawyer. You've obviously done what you intended. You've got me branded with this stupid green bracelet, which means I'm off-limits for the weekend. I get it. Party's over. Thanks for nothing."

She started to follow Stacey, intent on saying goodbye before returning to her friend's apartment.

Sawyer tightened his grip, halting her escape. "Where do you think you're going?"

"Back to Stacey's."

"No, you're not."

She paused. "What is your problem? It's obvious you don't like the idea of me hooking up." She lifted her arm, pointing to the green wristband. "By the way, you screwed yourself out of a good time too. You want me to leave, so I'm going."

Her voice had risen again, and several people standing close to them turned to look at her.

Sawyer put his arm around her waist and tugged her toward him—so close their bodies were connected from chest to toe. She tried to put some space between them, but Sawyer was too damn strong. The few muscles he hadn't acquired through a lifetime of ranch work seemed to have been found during his last seven years with the Coast Guard. The man was rock hard. Everywhere.

Arousal awoke in several parts of her body when she became aware of his erection pressing against her stomach.

"I'm not going to punish you for that outburst." His voice was deep and menacing—and God help her—sexy as hell. "You misunderstood my intent. So here's what I'm going to do."

He captured her gaze and held it. "I'm going to clarify for you in no uncertain terms what's happened. If you still try to leave after I've finished explaining, it will be a punishable offense. Do you understand?"

Sawyer had never talked to her like this. Never treated her with anything less than friendly, attentive courtesy. She wasn't sure how to respond to this commanding man, so she simply nodded.

"Good," he continued. "I claimed you as my submissive. You gave your consent to the host. That means I own you, Leah. For the next two days, you're mine. You aren't going anywhere except to my bed."

She stood spellbound for several moments, trying to process Sawyer's comments. He wanted her? In his bed? She closed her eyes, light-headed.

When she opened them again, he patiently studied her face. She shook her head. "I came here because I..." She paused. She couldn't tell him what she'd been thinking. Hell, she hadn't been able to admit it to herself for years. "We're friends, Sawyer. I really wanted—*needed*—a stranger. Someone who doesn't know me. I mean, chances are pretty damn good we'll run into each other again at home. That would be awkward. I was hoping to avoid that."

Sawyer frowned. "The last thing you need is someone who doesn't know you. Have you ever participated in a scene, submitted to someone? Anyone?"

She shook her head.

"Come with me."

He took her hand. She knew better than to resist. His face told her she wouldn't leave until he was ready to let her go. While she should be annoyed by his heavy-handedness, her body was on fire.

Like most girls in Compton Pass, she had carried a torch for Sawyer, though she had worked very hard to keep her ridiculous attraction to him a secret. After all, he was one of the infamous Compass brothers. Silas and Seth, the older brothers, had been legends by the time Leah entered high school and Sam and Sawyer, identical twin gods, sent most female hearts racing simply by claiming a nearby desk or saying hello in the hallway. At the time, she'd almost despised herself for her crush. She'd considered herself too practical, too intelligent to act like all the other love-struck girls in town.

Besides, she was smart enough to know nothing would ever come of her infatuation. She and Sawyer lived on two different planets as far as Compton Pass was concerned. Sawyer was the son of JD Compton, a powerful, wealthy rancher, whose quadruple-great-grandfather had founded the town. The Comptons were to Compton Pass what the Kennedys were to Martha's Vineyard. When they spoke, people listened.

Leah, on the other hand, was the only child of a waitress and some faceless sperm donor who hadn't stuck around beyond the morning after his romp with her mom. She was well versed in welfare and eviction notices and knew all too well how to stretch the almighty dollar. Sawyer had grown up on a sprawling ranch while she'd lived in a tiny apartment above the funeral home. As far as the class structure in Compton Pass was concerned, the Comptons fell into the *haves* category, while she and her mother lived firmly in the middle of the *have nots.*

When they reached the top of the massive staircase, Sawyer started down a long hallway. It was then she realized he was familiar with the house. "You've been here before."

He didn't reply until they stood outside a door. Sawyer took a key out of his pocket, unlocking it and gesturing for her to enter. The room was dark, except for the flicker of a single candle burning by the bed. He closed the door behind them. She heard the lock reengage and waited for him to turn on the lights.

He didn't.

"I've been here several times," he finally admitted. "Grey and I run in similar circles."

"With people who are into BDSM," she added, not bothering to make her words a question.

"Yes. Grey used to live in Portland, which is where I was first stationed. He moved to L.A. about the same time I was transferred to San Francisco, and we've kept up our acquaintance."

She jumped slightly when Sawyer gripped her waist. He spun her slowly, pushing until her back hit the door they'd entered. He stepped closer, completely surrounding her, caging her in.

Her breathing accelerated and her eyes drifted closed. She wondered what it would be like to kiss Sawyer. She'd always been too aware of him. Any time they were in a room together, she knew where he was, what he was doing, who he was talking to.

Now that they were alone together, his breath wafting across her face, the same breathless, heart-racing emotions that were so prevalent during her teenage years returned. She'd only ever felt this way about Sawyer, though she had no intention of telling him that. Besides being cocky, he was a Compton and she would never fit in his world.

"You look gorgeous tonight."

She wasn't sure how to respond. He thought she was gorgeous?

"I'm no Beth." Only half joking, she referred to the perky, perfect blonde cheerleader who'd bragged about losing her virginity to Sawyer. Leah had skipped gym class that day to keep from scratching the bitch's eyes out as Beth proceeded to go into graphic detail about the toe-tingling, earth-shattering experience.

Sawyer chuckled softly. "Thank God for that."

She frowned. What did that mean? Before she had a chance to ask, Sawyer changed the subject.

"Tell me why you came here tonight." It was a command, short and simple.

"I—" She faltered. She had some dark desires she'd planned to explore, but there was no way she could voice those to Sawyer.

"Tell me, Leah."

His mouth brushed her cheek as he spoke, and her knees went weak.

"I can't."

"Why not?"

"I don't want this with you."

His hand gently encompassed her neck, rubbing lightly, and even in the dim lighting, she sensed he was studying her reactions. "Liar."

Her backbone stiffened at his name-calling, even though it was one hundred percent accurate. "Is it so hard to believe that there's actually a woman in the world who doesn't feel the need to fall down at your feet?"

"Not so hard. Even though it is highly unlikely."

His face was pure mischief and before she could stop herself, she laughed. She appreciated his easygoing nature. It was one of the things she'd always admired and envied about Sawyer. While she'd spent most of her life wound up tighter than a spring, Sawyer was a go-with-the-flow kind of guy.

He stroked her face with the tips of his fingers. "That's a pretty laugh. I don't hear that enough from you."

"We've seen each other less than a dozen times the past seven years." Usually whenever Sawyer was home on leave, the two of them managed to meet up for lunch or dinner. They'd spend the evening catching up on life in general. Sawyer was the type of friend she could go months without speaking to, but once they were together it was like they'd never been apart.

"I know, but we've called and emailed and I got the letters and drawings from your students." Leah had started a pen-pal program between local men who'd joined the military and her kindergartners. The students drew pictures and she'd help them pen short accompanying messages. Sawyer never failed to write back to the kids. Once he sent a photo of himself in his uniform standing on the deck of a boat.

She smiled. "I hung your picture in my classroom. I had to break up a disagreement between two little girls when each of them insisted they were going to marry you when they grew up."

Sawyer laughed. "Nice to know I've still got a way with the ladies."

"You know Compton Pass. The more things change, the more they stay the same."

He nodded. "So what about you? Besides this shocking choice of attire and unexpected meeting, what's changed in your life? I assume you still haven't taken my suggestion and headed to Nashville to make it big as a songwriter."

His grip on her waist tightened slightly. She reached for his wrist, torn between pulling his too-provocative touch away or moving his hands higher. "That's not a very practical career option."

He rolled his eyes. "God. Still the same Leah. Both feet planted firmly on the ground."

"I like to think I'm too smart to believe in dreams that can't possibly come true. Fantasies don't pay the bills, money does."

It was obvious he didn't completely agree with her, but he didn't continue the argument.

Sawyer took her hand in his, lifting it and placing a soft kiss on her palm. She'd spent a lifetime wondering what it would be like to be with him, and while she'd always pictured hot, hard, amazing sex, she'd never anticipated his sweet caresses and humor would carry over to the bedroom as well. The rumors from the other girls back home had led her to believe he was an intense lover. She'd always wondered what it would be like to sleep with him. She'd fantasized about it far too many times since puberty hit.

"I'm not going to lie, Leah. I wanted you when we were in school together. I *really* wanted you."

She snorted. "Yeah right. I didn't see you beating down my door to ask me for a date."

He smiled ruefully. "You were a nice girl."

"So?"

"So I was a horny teenage boy. I wasn't looking for nice."

She glanced around the room. "Given our surroundings, it doesn't look like your requirements in female companionship have changed much."

He didn't deny her assertion. "Maybe not, but I think I may have gotten the best of both worlds tonight."

"How so?"

"I landed a nice girl who wants to be bad. That's better than riding the bull eight seconds, darlin'."

"You haven't scored yet, cowboy."

"No, but I'm about to."

"You think so?" she taunted.

He leaned closer, his hot breath tickling her face. "I know so."

Before he could say more, his cell rang. "Shit."

He didn't make a move.

"Aren't you going to answer it?"

He shook his head. "No."

The ringing stopped, but neither of them moved. Instead, they stood cheek-to-cheek, breathing in each other's scent.

Leah started to break the silence, but Sawyer's cell beat her to it as it rang once more.

"Fuck." He stepped back and took the phone out of his pocket. He started to switch it to silent, but glanced at the number. "It's Sam. We've been playing phone tag for weeks."

"You should answer it."

Sawyer pressed a button. "Dude. Really? Twice? I'm sort of busy..."

She grinned. She'd always been jealous of Sawyer and Sam's close relationship. An only child, she'd longed for siblings while she was growing up.

"Sam? What is it? Is Silas okay? Shit, I should have called. It's just..."

Leah looked up, concerned. Everyone at home knew about the injury Silas had received in an oil-rig explosion in Alaska. She'd seen Sawyer's oldest brother a few times since his return to Compton Pass. Enough to know that while his injuries were serious, they weren't life threatening. At least, she hadn't thought so.

Sawyer chuckled at Sam's response and set her mind at ease. He mouthed the words "butt dialed" to her, and she laughed.

"Twice? Talented ass you've got, bro."

"Give the poor guy a break," she teased him softly.

"I'll call you in the morning." Sawyer paused. "You're sure everything's good?"

Leah watched as Sawyer's grin grew. Clearly time and distance hadn't changed the close relationship between the brothers. She was glad.

Sawyer rolled his eyes. "Don't you worry about my cock, okay?"

Leah glanced down and raised her eyebrows suggestively at the unmistakable outline of his erection through his jeans. She licked her lips.

"Damn. Gotta go." He hung up the phone, silenced it and threw it on a chair in the corner. When he looked at her again, she forgot every reason, every concern she had about coming up to this room with Sawyer.

"Kiss me," she whispered.

He didn't pause, didn't waste a second considering her request. The moment the plea was issued, he was there—his lips claiming hers, conquering, possessing, overpowering her senses. His hands cupped her face, holding her in place as he plundered her mouth with his tongue. His teeth lightly nipped her lower lip and she moaned.

A shudder of need rumbled through her body as she grasped his waist, allowing the door at her back to support her weight as Sawyer gradually wiped every conscious thought from her mind. He was painting erotic, hungry pictures.

He broke off the kiss before she was ready. She moved her hands to his head, trying to draw him back to her. He didn't budge, didn't give in to her silent request.

Instead, he grasped her wrists. "Put your hands down."

She tried to shake off his grip, demand that he kiss her again, but his voice stopped her.

"Put them down, Leah."

Her eyes were starting to adjust to the dim light, and it allowed her to see his features more clearly. It was disconcerting—this near blindness—but it was also freeing. It made it easier to talk to him.

Sawyer slowly lowered her arms. "We're going to have to work on your inability to follow simple commands."

She scoffed, the sound escaping before she could think better. She'd never given any man power over her and, despite her desires, it was going to be hard to place herself in someone else's hands, especially Sawyer's. She'd come here looking for a stranger. Someone to indulge her fantasies and then disappear come morning.

"I see," he replied. "That resistance could be a problem."

"I told you that downstairs. You could have had your pick of any woman at this party. Why would you choose this power struggle? We know way too much about each other. There's no way it will work." Regret suffused her the moment she spoke. Despite what common sense was telling her, she wanted everything Sawyer could offer.

"You're wrong, and it's time you stopped evading my question. Why are you here?"

She couldn't find a suitable reply, one that would mask the truth sufficiently. Instead of trying, she simply repeated his words back to him. "Why are *you* here?"

"Leah." His tone was laced with warning.

"I'll answer. I swear I will, but it's not that easy for me. We're friends, Saw. But just because I've known you my entire life doesn't mean I'm comfortable revealing my most secret desires to you. Maybe if you went first..."

"I've missed you."

She frowned. "What?"

"We used to be really close. I've missed talking to you."

"I wrote and called. We did lunch whenever you were home."

He frowned. "A dozen meetings, broken up by phone calls, emails and those damn letters from the kids don't count. I missed hearing your voice, seeing your face every day."

He'd missed her. It was a sweet admission, one she hadn't expected to hear.

Back in school, she'd spent more time with Sam because of their class schedule. She and Sam were in the honors courses, while Sawyer tended to excel at the electives—gym, shop class. Their paths simply didn't cross that often during the day.

Instead, she and Sawyer had found time to hang out after school. Sawyer had been a regular in the diner where she worked and on days when she was off, they'd stroll around Compton Pass or roam around his family's ranch—just talking, dreaming about their futures.

In some ways, she'd found it easier to hang around Sam. He was less intimidating, less threatening to her well-being. Not that she'd ever been afraid of Sawyer. He was just too...too...

God. He was too everything.

"I missed you too."

Sawyer ran his finger along her neck, dragging it over her cleavage. Her eyes drifted closed, enjoying the warmth and sensuality of his simple touch. "Wanna know a secret?"

"What?"

"I always thought you liked Sam more. You two had a lot more in common than you and me."

She shook her head. "God no. I mean, Sam's a nice guy, but..." She paused, trying not to insult his twin.

"You don't want nice either, do you, Leah?"

"Of course I do."

He pinched her nipple. The rough touch was completely unexpected, yet it set off an earthquake of desire in her body. She threw her head back, hitting it against the door hard enough that she saw stars.

"Ouch."

Sawyer chuckled.

She narrowed her eyes. "That was mean."

He gently rubbed her scalp. "I know. Want me to do it again?"

She laughed at Sawyer's brash sense of fun. Her life had been too serious for too long. This time with him was a welcome reprieve, even if her expectations for the party had taken a dramatic turn from what she'd planned.

"You like pain?" he asked.

She let her silence answer the question. Hopefully it would be enough and again she was grateful for the darkness. A natural redhead, she had the tendency to blush often. Heat crept to her face as she considered all the things she wanted.

She took a deep breath. "I have a tendency to attract rather weak-willed men."

Sawyer didn't laugh, though she could tell he wanted to by his sardonic response. "I wonder why that is."

"If you're insinuating that *I'm* a control freak—"

"Sam calls you a force to be reckoned with."

She sighed. "I'm sure he does. I'm tired, Sawyer. So freaking exhausted."

"Of what?"

"I've been working since I was twelve. Do you know what I used my babysitting money for?"

Sawyer shook his head.

"It went toward paying the electric bill. As soon as I was old enough to wait tables with my mom, I started working at the diner. My mother insisted I was going to have a better life than her so whenever I wasn't waitressing, I was studying so I could get a scholarship to go to college. I had two jobs while I was at the university. After graduation, I went to Compton Pass and started teaching. I've spent my whole life working, trying to take charge of my destiny, so I didn't end up stuck in the damn diner forever."

Sawyer's hands engulfed her waist. She wasn't sure how that simple touch could convey so much, but it comforted her.

"I'm sick of being reliable, boring, a good girl."

"So what's the answer? You don't want to work anymore?" he asked.

She held up her hands. "Oh no, that's not what I'm saying. I love my teaching job. My kids are my life, and I couldn't leave them. I'm not tired of work, just my sex life. Everyone at home knows me. Knows I'm…"

"Sweet?" Sawyer supplied the word too quickly and she tried not to groan at his assessment. If one more person called her sweet tonight, she'd scream.

"Apparently, that trait tends to attract men who are looking for a mommy figure. I take care of kids all day. I can't come home at night and do more of the same."

She closed her eyes and tried to erase the image of her last three short-term boyfriends. Men content to let her decide where they would go for dinner, to lead the conversations, even to be the aggressor in bed. It was like they were afraid to touch her lest they offend her delicate disposition. Ugh.

"I'm still waiting for the BDSM explanation," Sawyer prompted.

She swallowed, and then decided a half truth was as good as a whole. "My college roommate, Stacey, called a few months ago to tell me about her new boyfriend. She was the girl you met downstairs."

Sawyer nodded, but didn't interrupt.

"She told me about Bill, about how he's a Dom. She talked about their sex life a little bit, and I realized she was describing my fantasies."

Sawyer grasped her hand. "You want someone else to take the reins in the bedroom."

She nodded. "Yes."

"Only in bed?"

Leah wondered if this would be a sticking point with Sawyer, then she decided that ultimately her answer didn't matter. Even though they were both from the same hometown, it wasn't like they saw each other often. Hell, Sawyer was away with the Coast Guard at least ninety-nine percent of the year.

This wasn't a date. It was a one-night stand. "My personality is pretty much set in cement. There's no way I can allow someone to manage my life outside of the bedroom."

He grinned, and she sensed her answer pleased him somehow. "So I guess there's only one question that remains."

"What's that?"

He grasped her hands and raised them. Holding them against the door by her head, he moved closer, trapping her lower body with his. She was completely at his mercy, and she loved it. She pressed her legs together in search of some sort of relief. She wasn't sure she'd ever been this horny in her life. With one quick aggressive motion, Sawyer sent her body spinning into orbit.

He moved nearer—something she would have thought impossible given their proximity. He rested his forehead against hers. "Why haven't you tried BDSM before?"

She shook her head. "I live in Compton Pass. Before tonight and with the exception of the exploits of you and your brothers, I would have called it the Vanilla Capital of the World."

Sawyer chuckled. "Guess you've never caught any rumors about the hands on the ranch. You are a pleasant surprise, Leah."

She snorted, the familiar teasing they used to indulge in returning. "Guess you should have been paying better attention in high school. Just think. I was right under your nose all those years, and you didn't even realize I was a girl."

He bent down, his hot breath teasing the sensitive skin of her cheek. "You're wrong. I noticed you."

She licked her suddenly dry lips as his tongue darted out to touch her throat lightly.

"Your heart's racing," he whispered.

She nodded once.

"Scared?"

She frowned. "No."

"Nervous?"

Hell yeah. Unfortunately her pride was as strong as her curiosity. "No."

He kissed her softly. "Liars get punished."

She swallowed deeply, wondering if punishment would be such a bad thing if Sawyer was administering it. Then she decided not to test him...yet. "Maybe a little nervous."

"Are you excited?"

Christ, that seemed to be an understatement in regard to her current state. She was keyed up, enthralled, and far too eager for what came next. When she'd climbed the stairs with Sawyer, she'd been equal parts annoyed and terrified. Given the stories Stacey had shared about her experiences with Bill and the few things she'd seen downstairs, Sawyer's treatment of her had been far kinder than she'd expected. He'd talked to her, given her a chance to put her thoughts in order, while slowly accustoming her to his touches, his soft kisses, even the pinch. He was gentling her like she'd watched him do with the horses on his family's ranch.

"I want you," she whispered.

"Good." He took a step back and pressed on her shoulders, applying downward pressure until she had no choice but to kneel. He ran a single finger along her face. Without a word, he managed to get her into a subservient position. Arousal dampened her panties. So far, so good. Her body temperature rose rapidly.

"Open my pants," he said. "Take my cock out. Run your hand along it, but don't touch it with your mouth."

It was too dark in the room and suddenly she wished there was more light. She would like to see Sawyer's handsome face and the hard flesh he'd pressed against her stomach.

She unfastened his zipper. Tugging on the denim, she dragged it to his knees.

He went commando.

So hot.

She grasped his erect cock, surprised by the heat emanating from him. He was long and thick and her mouth watered at the thought of taking him between her lips. She wished she could find relief, and she wondered if Sawyer would notice her touching herself. Of course he would. He saw everything where she was concerned.

She recalled her purpose, tried to suppress her immediate needs, and forged on. Wrapping her hand around him, she studied his girth as she stroked him. Leah marveled at Sawyer's command of his own body as she touched him. While she felt like a kettle about to boil over, he stood in stoic silence as she explored his flesh. The devil in her prompted her to ratchet up the play, to try to provoke a response. She cupped his balls, squeezing slightly before gripping the base of his cock harder. With her other hand, she teased the mushroom-shaped head, rubbing her finger through the drops of pre-come she found there. She longed to taste him, to make him groan. She closed her hand tighter as she dragged it along his turgid flesh.

He didn't make a sound as he lifted his hands from her shoulders, placing them on either side of her head. His fingers tangled into her hair, and she closed her eyes when the pressure built. As she increased the force on his cock, his hands tightened—her only hint that he was as captivated by this moment as she was.

"Pull my hair," she whispered, her tone pleading.

He complied, increasing his grip until she shuddered at the delicious pain. She was slowly going out of her mind with desire. Her pussy fluttered and her nipples ached for the same rough touch. She leaned forward and opened her mouth, pulling his cock toward her lips.

She was a hairsbreadth away from taking him into her mouth when Sawyer forcefully pulled her head back, depriving her of her treat.

"I told you not to touch me with your mouth."

"Please," she whispered. She needed him to make her feel alive. She was tired of being alone, of being an empty shell.

His hands cupped her face and tilted it until she had no choice but to look at him. "Give yourself to me."

She faltered. "What?"

"You haven't given up control yet. You're still fighting me. Trying to call the plays. Do you believe I'll make this good for you?"

She nodded. She didn't even need to think about his question. She trusted Sawyer implicitly.

"Then prove it."

As she looked into his dark eyes, the tiny part of her Sawyer had claimed when they were kids grew. This wasn't good. She was here to fulfill the needs of her body, not her heart.

She hadn't come into this club tonight looking for love. She'd been searching for a sexual fantasy. That was all.

She put away her silly, soft emotions and forced herself to return to the original plan. Suddenly what had been so embarrassing to say earlier came easier. It was certainly less revealing than confessing that she was completely infatuated with him. "Tie me up. Render me helpless. Spank me, use me, take me hard."

Make me feel something.

God, make me feel anything.

He paused for a moment and she feared she'd gone too far. Then he grinned. "Yep. Better than eight seconds."

Chapter Two

Sawyer's head swam as he considered Leah's racy invitation. He'd spent every minute in her presence struggling to keep a cool head...and body. He wasn't sure what exactly it was about Leah Hollister that captured his attention and held it so tightly, but he'd watched the fiery redhead with far too much lust for years.

She'd always been a sweet girl and a good friend to him. Once when he'd had the flu during their junior year, she'd come to visit and snuck him a dessert from the diner. After she left, JD had claimed she was a rose in a field of dandelions. That image had stuck in Sawyer's mind.

When his gaze landed on her beautiful face downstairs, he'd vowed the night wouldn't end without her tied to his bed.

Sawyer looked down at Leah's upturned face, as she waited patiently for his next command. His too-hard cock thickened even more. She was giving herself to him. He wouldn't abuse her faith in him.

She licked her lips once more, her gaze dropping to his cock. He grinned. She really wanted this, wanted him. He moved closer, missing her touch, her warmth. "Take me in your mouth."

Leah obeyed without hesitation. Her hunger was evident when she took him to the back of her throat in two deep passes.

He held her still as she moved quickly, her motions almost erratic in her haste to consume him. "Easy, rose. We have all night."

He grasped her long auburn hair tighter, relishing the softness. With a firm grip, he directed her movements, slowing down each entry and retreat. While his cock was ready to blow, he wasn't about to give in to that need. Tonight was about Leah and letting her explore her untried fantasies.

However, it seemed likely they'd *both* be granted a wish or two. He'd had more than his fair share of sexy dreams about the woman currently blowing him into oblivion.

When his cock brushed the back of her throat again, she swallowed the head. It was time to call a halt before he passed the point of no return. He took a step away, repressing a groan when Leah followed his motion, refusing to free him.

"Stop."

She released him instantly, frowning. "Why?"

He lightly tapped her nose. "Because I said so, Leah. You have to trust me to make this good for you. For both of us."

She licked her lips. It took all the strength in Sawyer's body not to say to hell with it and shove his cock back into her sexy mouth. He'd give his left nut to come down her throat. She offered him a seductive smile that told him she knew exactly what she was doing to him.

"You're a bad girl." He removed his pants.

Her grin widened, and she didn't bother to deny his accusation.

"You know what happens to cock teases, don't you?"

She shook her head slowly, not bothering to show an ounce of contrition.

"They get spanked."

Her gaze never left his—never revealed an ounce of fear. She was perfect. Spirited and strong, yet soft and willing. Is this what had attracted him to her all these years? Had his inner dominant sensed the generous woman beneath the independent exterior? Leah was a survivor and as always, he ached with the need to protect her.

Sawyer bent slightly and placed his hands beneath her arms, helping her to her feet. The slightest shiver racked her body as she allowed him to lift her.

He looked at her, concerned. "Before we go any further, there are some rules we need to establish."

"Okay."

"If things get too heavy or you need a time-out, say yellow and I'll stop what I'm doing. We'll discuss what's happening, slow things down to give you time to process."

She nodded.

"Don't just nod. Let me hear it, Leah."

"Yellow."

He continued. "If I do something that hurts you or that you absolutely don't want, use the word red. As soon as you say that, I'll stop and I won't do it again. Ever."

"Red means stop."

He brushed a stray tendril of hair away from her cheek. He found it virtually impossible to keep himself from touching her. "But be warned, Leah. If you say red, there's no going back. Red is forever and saying it three times is the equivalent of three strikes, you're out."

"What do you mean?"

"I mean BDSM isn't for the fainthearted. If you feel the need to keep stopping, there's a good chance this lifestyle isn't for you. There's nothing wrong with that. Don't do anything tonight simply because you hope it will please me or because of that damned pride of yours."

She rolled her eyes, but he wouldn't be deterred. "I mean it.

There's no shame in admitting *I don't like this*. You're new to the concept, and you planned this trip so you could explore. That's what we're going to do. Test your boundaries, maybe uncover some kinks."

She grinned. "Never really thought of myself as a kinky girl. I like it."

He didn't laugh, though she meant her joke to be funny. "That's what I'm trying to explain to you, Leah. You could just as easily discover you aren't. There's nothing wrong with that."

She sobered up. "I understand what you're saying."

"There's only one thing you could do tonight that would truly anger me and that's lie about what you want. What we do together is meant to bring you pleasure. It's not something for you to endure. Don't be afraid to use those words. I'd be far more annoyed if you let me do something that caused you genuine pain or fear and you said nothing. Do you understand?"

"Yes."

Sawyer took a deep breath. He'd never wanted—needed—a night to be perfect. He'd waited a lifetime to get Leah Hollister into his bed, and he was determined to make this weekend one she would never forget.

"Get undressed."

She paused and, for a moment, he feared she was having second thoughts. "Leah?"

She looked down. "You may have to help me with this damn corset. Stacey tied it so tight, I can barely breathe. There's no way I can escape the torture chamber on my own."

He frowned when he realized she was suffering. "Turn around."

She blinked at his harsh tone, but he didn't give her time to respond. Instead he gripped her shoulders and twisted her so he could tackle the knot at the base of her spine. She wasn't lying about the tension.

"Don't ever wear a corset this tight again. It's dangerous."

Leah didn't reply, but he didn't miss her deep sigh of relief when he loosened the stiff material. Reaching around her, he unfastened the hooks, enjoying the sensation of holding her in his arms. Leah rested her head on his shoulder and again he was overwhelmed by her innate trust in him. She lifted her arms at his silent bidding, and he peeled the leather away from her body. Even in the dim lighting, he could see the deep ridges the corset left in her pale skin. She'd obviously spent the past few hours in discomfort.

He touched them softly, not pulling away when Leah jerked slightly. She glanced over her shoulder at him, but he couldn't look away from her back. In the past, he'd seen similar marks on other lovers. For some reason, those images hadn't bothered him. With Leah, the defender within reared his ugly head and roared.

"Don't ever hurt yourself like this again, Leah."

She shuddered at his harsh tone, but he didn't bother to soften it. He'd tried to ease her into the situation, but it was time to give her a glimpse of what she'd signed on for.

"Take off the skirt."

Sawyer's hands were balled into fists as he struggled to get a grip. To center himself. In the past, he'd found it very easy to direct his inner dominant. That wasn't the case with Leah. He wanted too much, too fast. If he didn't calm down, he was going to fuck up everything. She'd obviously taken more than her fair share of lame lovers in the past. He refused to see his name added to that list because he couldn't get his shit together.

Leah unzipped her skirt and shimmied the material over

her rounded hips. Mercifully, she wasn't one of those paper-thin women afraid to eat more than two bites of a meal. Leah had meat on her bones in all the right places—generous hips, an ass that begged to be squeezed, large breasts. She was equal parts soft and firm and made for fucking. His ideal image of feminine beauty.

Her back was still turned, but Sawyer was in no hurry to rush his first perusal of her bare flesh. He soaked in the sight, committing each tempting curve to memory.

Once he'd gotten his fill, he said, "Face me."

Leah responded instantly, and he was blown away by her obedience. Jesus. She was perfection incarnate. An Amazon at heart, she stood before him, refusing to look away as his gaze drifted over her body. He didn't bother to hide his appraisal or his approval.

"Beautiful," he whispered.

She smiled gratefully, though her lips parted as if she would protest.

He narrowed his eyes in warning. "You're gorgeous, Leah, and I intend to spend the rest of the evening proving that fact to you."

"Tonight isn't turning out as I expected."

He led her to the bed. Sitting on the edge, he gestured for her to join him. "What were you expecting?"

She shrugged. "I figured I'd meet some bossy, leather-clad guy who'd pull me into the bedroom, tie me up and do unspeakable things to me."

Sawyer laughed. "Jesus. And you still came?"

She crinkled her nose ruefully. "Stupid, right? Guess that goes to show my level of desperation."

Sawyer could understand Leah's reasons for exploring the

D/s concept, but he was disturbed by how blindly she'd walked into this house party. It made his blood run cold to think of another man initiating her into the lifestyle without knowing her. If Leah had ended up with the wrong sort of Dom, her experience would have been disastrous.

Again, the overwhelming need to protect her—this time from herself—bubbled up. "Your friends were wrong to bring you here without preparing you a little better in terms of what to expect."

Sawyer stood. "Lie down on the mattress. In the middle."

He had a whole list of things he planned to do with and to Leah, but he refused to rush. They would start off slow and build. After all, the night was still young.

Leah climbed to the center of the bed and lay on her back. He leaned over, positioning her arms above her head. "You've never tried any kind of bondage?"

"I dated a guy once who asked me to tie him up. I tried it, but it felt sort of icky and wrong. I was bored and couldn't wait for it to be over."

He kissed her forehead. "That's because you were on the wrong end of the straps." As he spoke, he tugged on ties attached to the headboard. Leah glanced up when he gripped her wrists. Some deeply engrained self-preservation instinct made her fight him briefly, but Sawyer didn't give her a chance to escape. Instead he tightened his hold and moved faster. In less than a minute he had both of her hands secured together.

Leah tested the strength of her bonds.

"You won't break free, rose."

Moving to the foot of the bed, Sawyer grabbed her left ankle before she could guess his purpose. He secured it to the footpost, and then did the same to the right. Standing at the bottom edge of the mattress, he studied her outstretched state.

She was completely open to him, helpless and at his mercy. His dreams of Leah were about to come true in a single night.

She squirmed and fought briefly against her bondage, but she didn't protest and she didn't say either of her safe words. She narrowed her eyes when he continued to stare at her in hungry silence.

"I don't think I trust that look."

He grinned. "I'm like a kid in a candy store. Not sure what to do first."

"Yeah, well, hurry. I have a bit of a sweet tooth myself."

Sawyer fought the urge to rip off his shirt and join her on the bed. "Ever heard the expression *topping from the bottom*?"

She shook her head.

"I didn't think so. Let's just say you're doing it a lot, and it's not a good thing."

Leah's gaze drifted along his body. Each glance a caress. He tugged at the hem of his T-shirt and pulled the material over his head.

Leah's softly muttered "fuck" and widened eyes were the best compliment he'd ever received.

After getting his first tattoo after graduation with Sam, Sawyer had decided he liked the look of them. He'd added a strip of barbed wire to his left bicep and the Coast Guard insignia on the right pec. She couldn't see the large one on his back—the one he shared with his brothers—and something compelled Sawyer to turn around to see what she thought of it.

Instead, he stood still and let her look her fill.

"Sawyer, I…"

There was only one word to describe Leah. Horny. She was squirming like a worm on a hook. Her body was flushed, and the temperature in the room had definitely spiked. He'd purposely stalled, letting the helplessness of being bound permeate her consciousness. She may be new to the concept, but she clearly liked it.

He thought about tying her to the St. Andrew's Cross hanging on the wall behind him or facedown over the spanking bench by the bed. His mind raced with all the ways he wanted Leah at his mercy and suddenly two days didn't seem long enough.

Leah's gaze never left his body. She was a ticking time bomb and he couldn't wait to watch her explode.

He ran his hand along his erection. The action was meant to tease her, but it was helping him as well. He'd never failed to hold off his release for hours as he brought his partner to orgasm after orgasm. He wasn't entirely sure he'd be able to wait that long with Leah.

She'd accused him of never asking her out, but he'd actually planned to invite her to the prom their senior year. When he'd told his father, something JD said stopped him.

His father shared his love of hard sex and dominance, though they'd never said the words aloud. Growing up, he'd heard stories about his dad through eavesdropping on the ranch hands. At first, he'd worried about his desire for rough play, afraid of hurting girls, but hearing other men—even his dad—shared those urges had set his mind at ease. He and his father were kindred spirits. Vicky liked to joke that the fruit hadn't fallen far from the tree when he was born.

When he had told his dad who he was going to ask to the dance, JD had simply nodded, pierced him with a narrow-eyed look and said, "Son, there are some girls in this world who will leave you wanting a hell of a lot more than a tumble in the hayloft. Leah is one of those. Keep that in mind."

His father's warning confused him. He'd decided not to

tempt fate. He'd definitely planned to have sex with Leah after the dance, but he couldn't promise her more than that. His plans for after graduation began and ended with getting the hell out of Dodge. Instead he'd invited Beth to the dance.

Since then, his trips home had only been quick visits and indulging in an affair with Leah had still felt wrong. He was in the Coast Guard and had no plans to stay in Compton Pass, but Leah wouldn't be happy living anywhere else. He couldn't suggest a long-distance relationship because it would never have been enough for him, and he couldn't ask her to give up her job to come with him.

Looking at Leah now, Sawyer realized his father had been right to issue the warning. The timing had been wrong for them before.

He crawled onto the mattress, covering her body with his.

Leah's breathing accelerated.

"Easy," he whispered.

"I've never felt like this."

"What do you mean?"

She closed her eyes. "I'm coming out of my skin."

He grinned. "Well, guess that's the only option left since I've already gotten you out of your clothes."

She pierced him with her bright blue eyes. "I thought Doms were supposed to be strict and stern and serious all the time."

He shook his head. "Remind me to beat your ass later. You really should have done *some* research about BDSM before coming here tonight."

She laughed at his threat. Sawyer struggled to keep a smile from his face as well. Leah was fun, easy to be with. She was taking his previous experiences in the bedroom and turning them on their ear.

"What? I'm the queen of living on the wild side," she teased. "After all, I risk life and limb every single day I enter that classroom filled with snotty-nosed, whiny, pee-pee-pants five-year-olds."

Sawyer winced. "Damn. I guess this party looked like a cakewalk compared to that."

She sobered up. "Maybe so, but don't let the fact I lack the self-preservation gene keep you from indulging in that spanking. I sort of like the sound of that."

"Christ. Topping from the bottom again. You're definitely going to be punished. Later."

Unable to resist any longer, he kissed her. For several moments, he merely worshiped her lips—letting himself sample her taste, her sweet scent, her soft cries. Even without the use of her hands, Leah managed to make herself more than a mere recipient. She pressed harder, trying to deepen the kiss. When his tongue reached out, hers was there—meeting him halfway. Twice, she nipped his lower lip in her desire for more.

She thrashed against his as much as the ties would allow, and Sawyer was hard-pressed not to plunge into her body, to give in to the needs coursing through his veins. When the last vestige of his control stretched taut, he pulled away.

Leah protested. "No."

She was still trying to manage the situation. Regardless of what she was looking for in bed, she wouldn't give up the reins easily. Years of being forced to fend for herself would die hard.

He moved along her body until his lips were poised at the tip of one beautiful breast. He bit her nipple in warning. "Don't say no to me, Leah. You won't like what happens when you do."

She narrowed her eyes and started to issue a set-down. He cut off any complaint she might make by biting the other nipple—harder.

She gasped, but otherwise remained silent.

"Good girl."

Her hands clenched into fists, and she struggled against the straps binding her. He was purposely goading her. Suddenly it seemed Sunday would come too soon. He'd always dreamed of Leah, her face reappearing to him many times in the past. During long, lonely nights when he was on board his boat, he'd close his eyes and it was the image of Leah who came to him, talked to him, kept him company.

This weekend wouldn't be enough. The realization hit him like a blow to the gut, but he dismissed the thought before it could take root. His life was in a state of flux right now and he was in no position to consider entering a committed BDSM relationship. No matter how much he wanted one with Leah. He'd been struggling with re-upping for another stint with the Coast Guard. While his decision to resign had been made— mostly—he wasn't ready to add anything else to the mix.

After several moments of tugging on the ties, struggling for freedom, his patience was rewarded. Leah stilled beneath him.

She hadn't said either of her safe words. In the past, he reminded subs of the rules whenever they might be in over their heads. He couldn't do the same for Leah. For one thing, he didn't think she'd appreciate him questioning her ability to take care of herself and for another, he was afraid the reminder would prompt her to use one. He didn't want to stop.

Grasping her right breast in his palm, he bent his head to kiss away the sting. Sucking the tight nub into his mouth, he gradually increased the pressure until Leah cried out. Releasing it with a pop, he turned and delivered the same touch to her other breast.

Leah's resistance to the bondage began again, but this time the tenor of her battle was different. She wasn't fighting to be released. She was aching for leverage, spurring him on and silently begging for more. Her hips lifted. The hair of her pussy brushed against his stomach. The action reminded Sawyer of one more thing.

Raising his head, he waited until her gaze met his. "There's another rule, Leah. You aren't allowed to come until I give you permission."

She didn't resist this decree like he'd expected. She was out of her head with need, and he liked the look on her.

"That won't be a hard one to follow," she whispered.

He stopped, confused. "Why do you say that?"

His question jarred her and she blinked rapidly. A slight blush tinged her cheeks. "No reason."

It was a lie. The Dom in him reared in the face of her dishonesty. His fingers itched to pull her over his lap and show her what happened to subs who told fibs. He didn't move.

"I'm going to give you one more chance to answer my question. This time I expect to hear the truth." He didn't verbalize the consequences facing her. It was evident by her stricken expression she knew they would be severe.

She closed her eyes and turned her head slightly away from him. "I—" She licked her lips.

"Look at me, Leah."

She shook her head. "No. This is uncomfortable enough—"

He placed his hand on her chin and turned her face to him. "Open your eyes, rose. Don't you see? There's nothing awkward between us."

She lifted her eyelids, her clear blue eyes catching his gaze and holding. "I've never had an orgasm."

He didn't respond immediately. Tried to give himself a minute to process the meaning. Given her confession about taking weak lovers, he wasn't surprised, but... "You mean with another man?"

She bit her lower lip. "Ever. I have a tendency to think too much in bed."

He fought the urge to laugh. He loved her constantly whirling brain, but he could see how it would cause her some trouble—especially if none of her previous lovers had been able to make her mindless in bed.

There was something else though that bothered him. "What about when you masturbate?" Surely she had a vibrator. She was a vivacious woman with a more-than-healthy sex drive.

She shook her head and her blush deepened. "I get close, but then...it's like something inside me shuts down. I've read a few articles on the subject, and it's not really that uncommon in some women."

He considered her *shut down* comment and knew immediately what the problem was. The answer seemed obvious, but apparently Leah hadn't figured it out yet.

She mistook his silence and before he could say anything else, she sighed heavily. "This is going to be a deal-breaker, isn't it?"

He couldn't help it. This time he chuckled. He couldn't wait to show her everything she'd been missing. "My previous rule stands. You aren't allowed to come without permission."

She frowned, the action causing the cutest crinkles to mar her forehead. "But—"

"An orgasm is the ultimate form of losing control. You won't even allow yourself that power. It doesn't matter, Leah. You're going to give it to me."

She shuddered at his proclamation, but she didn't refute it.

The time for conversation had ended. From this point on,

the only words uttered would be commands. He had her exactly where he wanted her and nothing would deter him now.

He moved lower, positioning himself between her outstretched legs. The sweet scent of her arousal drove him crazy and he refused to deny himself a taste any longer. Bending, he placed his lips around her clit and sucked strongly on the tiny button. Leah reacted as if she'd been struck by lightning, her hips thrashing roughly.

He gripped her waist in his hands to hold her still and repeated the motion. Leah cried out, her soft voice driving him to crank up the play. Nipping at her clit, he slowly applied more pressure, interested in seeing exactly how high Leah's threshold for pain was. Each time he clenched harder, she yelled louder, begging, pleading with him for more. His muscles tightened and he prayed for strength. As her need grew, so did his. His cock was aching, ready to explode.

The skin on her thighs grew slick with arousal. Sawyer pushed two fingers inside her cunt, and Leah shuddered hard. He'd hoped the added sensation would drive her over the edge, but Leah hadn't lied about her problem. Her mind and body waged a violent war against each other. She instantly calmed.

Her breathing came rapidly. "Fuck," she muttered. He glanced up. Tears formed in the corner of her eyes. She had to come, but something was holding her back and causing her a fair amount of pain along the way.

"I, I w-want…"

Her voice died as she struggled to speak.

"I know, Leah." He pulled his fingers out and returned with three. He slammed them to the hilt, and her body reared up. He placed his palm against her stomach, applying enough pressure to keep her still. He bent over and sucked roughly on her clit as he finger-fucked her.

Once again, Leah climbed, her pussy muscles reaching for that last bit of glory. When it seemed inevitable, he lifted his head. "Come, Leah. Come for me, baby."

Her face was contorted with need and pain and when he thought she'd achieve that final goal, her body shut down. A lone tear trickled down her cheek, and Sawyer's heart ached for her. He stood.

Leah panicked. "Oh God, no. I'm sorry. Please don't stop."

He stilled. "I'm not leaving, rose. I need a few things. Don't move." It was a preposterous statement—she was strapped to the bed—but his brain was focused on only one thing at the moment.

Reaching into a box at the foot of the bed, he gathered up his tools. In the past, he'd called them toys, but tonight, they were going to help him conquer Leah and her control demon. Tonight, he was going to claim the woman, make her his.

Glancing at the bed, he heard JD's words in his head. *Some women will leave you wanting more than a tumble in the hayloft.* Leah certainly fit that bill. He grinned as the game plan changed. This weekend adventure had stretched into something more.

If Sawyer played his cards right tonight, they could be embarking on a long-term engagement.

Chapter Three

Leah repressed a shiver when Sawyer returned. There was a possessiveness in his gaze that hadn't been there before. When he'd gotten off the bed, she feared she'd pissed him off when she hadn't been able to come. She'd dated plenty of men who took her inability to orgasm as some sort of personal affront to their so-called manhood.

Obviously Sawyer was different if the look on the face of the determined man climbing on the bed was anything to go by. She should have realized he wouldn't be easily deterred. He was a Compton and they loved a challenge. Sawyer's serious expression told her he was a man on a mission.

A small part of her was thrilled by his tenacity, but the larger, more practical side of her feared this night was going to end like so many others before—with her faking an orgasm. It wasn't until Sawyer knelt between her legs again that she realized his hands were full.

"What's all that?"

He grinned, but didn't respond. Instead, he lifted a rabbit vibrator from the mattress. She owned a similar one herself—not that it had done much more than leave her even more frustrated on lonely nights, but she didn't mention that to Sawyer.

He placed the toy at the opening of her body and worked it in. While the sensation of it entering her was similar to what she'd experienced at home, she had to admit there was something extra sexy and naughty about Sawyer wielding the vibrator. Fully lodged, he lined up the clit stimulator and turned it on low. She jerked though she'd anticipated the familiar motion.

She'd only gotten close to coming with the toy when it was on high gear, but before she could offer the advice, Sawyer leaned forward until his lips were at her breasts.

She groaned when he took her nipple into his mouth, the suction hard enough it sent spikes of arousal straight to her pussy.

"So good," she whispered.

He didn't respond. Instead he continued sucking and biting until she thought she'd go mad. When he raised his head at last, she expected him to turn his attention to her other breast. He lifted his hand and the glimmer of something metallic caught her eye.

"What—?" Before she could finish her question, Sawyer snapped something onto her taut nipple, the clamp biting into her sensitive flesh.

She cried out at the pleasurable pain and fought to close her legs around the vibrator still teasing her pussy. The damn ties at her ankles held her open, helpless to take what she needed. "God. Please."

She wasn't sure what she wanted, but something had to give or she was likely to spontaneously combust.

Sawyer remained quiet, his mouth issuing the same beautiful torture to her other breast. His lips, teeth and tongue worked on her left nipple until it stood erect enough for his fastener.

Once both clamps were in place, Sawyer cranked up the speed—one notch—on the vibrator.

She trembled, gasping for breath, as a thin sheen of sweat

covered her body.

Sawyer knelt between her knees. His gaze traveled along her body, studying the havoc he was wreaking.

"Help me," she whispered. "Please."

He smiled at her. "Who's in charge of your body, Leah?"

His question pierced. The selfish, prideful part of her soul couldn't give him the answer he sought.

Her silence dragged on too long. She expected Sawyer to become annoyed, angry. Instead, he grabbed an extra pillow. Lifting her hips, he placed the pillow beneath her rear end. The action tightened the pull of the straps at her ankles.

He moved forward, something long and dark in his hand. She forgot to breathe when he raised the blindfold and placed it over her eyes. "You're thinking too much, Leah. You're watching my face and letting what you perceive as my feelings drive your reactions. I'm not part of this equation. This is all about you."

"I can't..." Her voice wavered. She couldn't what? She'd tried to tell herself for years that her inability to climax was physical, but that was a lie. For her, it was all mental, all a damn head game.

Sawyer's breath tickled her ear. "Of course you can," he whispered. "You need to let go."

Easier said than done. She sucked in some much-needed air. Without her vision, her other senses kicked in. Sawyer walked to the foot of the bed, releasing the ties around her ankles.

Relief suffused her. Maybe now she could work with that vibrator. She closed her legs, ready to grind her hips to force the vibrator deeper when Sawyer's hands clamped around her ankles.

"Don't move unless I tell you to."

"But I—"

"God dammit, Leah." His voice took on that stern tone she'd expected from a Dom. "I know *exactly* what you need. Now hold still."

She froze, his command driving her arousal even higher.

"Jesus." Sawyer muttered softly and she wished she could see his face, so she could figure out what he found so amazing.

"You really are a sub," he added. The admiration soaked into her skin like balm on a burn. She'd always suspected that truth and now Sawyer had confirmed it for her. She sighed, oddly relieved.

He retained his grip on her ankles as he moved to the side of the bed. Lifting them, he continued pulling on her legs until her feet were next to each of her bound hands. Good thing she was flexible.

Apparently there were more fasteners on the headboard. Sawyer secured her ankles near her hands. She was bent in half and trussed tighter than a calf in the rodeo. This was what she got for taking up with a cowboy.

Sawyer returned to his previous position, and this time she could only imagine the bird's-eye view he had of her female parts. Her hips were elevated by the pillow, and her legs tied shoulder-width apart, leaving her open for his perusal. He was getting the grand tour of not only her pussy, but God help her, her ass.

She should be mortified, but the extreme helplessness of her new position was weaving its insidious way through every part of her body. She closed her eyes behind the blindfold. A calm she'd never experienced came over her.

Sawyer must have sensed the difference. "Who's in control of your body?"

Her mind whirled, battling against what was right and what was true. The feminist in her shouted it was *her* body, but she wasn't so certain that was the reality any longer. Sawyer was a master lover, while she lived in novice land. He was provoking sensations she'd never dreamed about.

She parted her lips to give him an answer, but Sawyer cut her off with a hard slap on her lifted ass. "Too long. You should be able to answer that question without thinking about it."

She cried out when he placed three more hard spanks against her bare bottom, the unfamiliar sensation growing as his slaps grew in intensity. She'd never been spanked before. Not even as a child when she had been naughty. No one had ever lifted a finger to punish her. Something told her she wouldn't have liked it if it had come from any other man. His slaps continued, varying in strength, each one covering a slightly different area.

Soon, the pain morphed into something unique as her pussy clenched against the vibrator lodged in her pussy. She moaned as a rumble of pleasure shook her entire body. Sawyer swatted her again, his hand landing slightly below the toy. She jerked, her pussy clamping.

"God," she cried. "Harder. More."

Sawyer continued to spank her, giving her something so indescribably amazing she was light-headed, dizzy.

She protested when he stopped, but Sawyer softly shushed her and moved to her side. "I need to take off these clamps. It's going to hurt."

She couldn't imagine the removal could be any worse than his powerful spanking. She was wrong. Sawyer told her to take a deep breath, but even that didn't prepare her for the agonizing rush of blood flowing back to her nipples.

The initial throbbing gave way to a flood of pleasurable

sensations, the feelings new, unique, incredible. Her pussy muscles took over, working against the vibrator until Leah saw stars.

Sawyer lightly rubbed her breasts until the pain subsided, then knelt at her ass. Apart from the brief, incomplete blowjob earlier, she hadn't touched Sawyer's cock. His erection had looked almost painfully hard, and she wondered how he was managing to hold off.

She hungered for him. Craved him. The toy wasn't enough. It would never be enough for her. "I need you inside me." Her words couldn't be misconstrued as anything other than what they were—begging.

Sawyer ran his finger around the edge of the vibrator, rubbing the wetness he found there into her clit. The touch sent a spasm through her body.

"Please."

Sawyer didn't respond. Instead, his finger gathered more moisture. This time, he dragged the wetness to her anus.

"Shit," she hissed.

He ran his index finger around the edge several times before pushing in to the first knuckle. She shuddered, and he paused. She was growing accustomed to his slight starts and stops. Every time he introduced something new, he hesitated briefly to give her time to think about it. He was waiting for her to use one of her words. She wouldn't.

Something cool hit her anus and she jerked.

"Lube," Sawyer said.

He squeezed more lubrication inside and used it to ease his finger's path into her ass. There was the slightest bite of discomfort to his entry, but it quickly changed into something hot, sexy, incredible.

She liked her pleasure laced with pain. Leah had hidden those thoughts from previous lovers because it seemed wrong, unnatural. Now she realized she hadn't explored them before because she hadn't truly trusted those men to protect her.

Sawyer was the only man she'd ever allow to touch her this way. In a single night, he was ruining her for all other men.

God. How was she going to return to her real life on Sunday? How could she see his identical twin, Sam, around Compton Pass and not ache with sadness over missing Sawyer. This wasn't supposed to happen. She'd simply planned to get away, have some awesome sex, and then go home stronger, wiser.

She was screwed. Literally and figuratively.

"Still with me, Leah?"

"Yes." She was—more than he realized.

Once his finger was lodged in her ass, Sawyer cranked the speed on the vibrator to high.

Leah hadn't expected the sudden change. It drove all her fears away in a red-hot instant. Her body shifted into overdrive when Sawyer pulled his finger almost completely out of her ass before driving it in again.

She screamed, her pussy pulsing against the vibrator. She was so close. So fucking close.

"Need. More. You." Each word came out in a separate pant. "Inside. Me."

"Are you on the Pill?"

She nodded. "Yes. Please, Sawyer. Now."

Sawyer's finger was still lodged in her ass, but he wasn't moving anymore. "Who's in control of your body, Leah?"

"You." The confession fell from her lips without a moment's hesitation or thought. It was simply the truth.

He pulled off her blindfold and captured her gaze. "I'm going to make sure you never forget that."

The finger and vibrator disappeared before she could respond, but Leah didn't have a chance to miss either as Sawyer placed the head of his cock at her opening. "Come inside me. With nothing between us."

He hadn't put on a condom. She didn't care. She was protected, and she trusted Sawyer implicitly. He would never hurt her. At least, not more than she could stand. That sexy realization caused more juices to flow, easing Sawyer's path into her body. Her earlier blowjob had proved he was large, but now she was appreciating how much so. Within seconds, he was as deep as their bodies would allow, filling every inch of her.

He untied her ankles, though he kept them up with his shoulders. "You ready for this?"

She grinned as she nodded, the brief assent the only permission he needed.

Sawyer retreated from her body and returned with more force than a two-ton wrecking ball. Over and over he plunged into her body. He didn't hold back any of the strength he possessed. His claiming was so much like him—tough, powerful, demanding, beautiful.

She accepted every hard thrust as her rightful due. Sawyer may not have pursued her in high school, but she was determined he'd crave her now. Recognize the woman she'd grown up to be.

She tightened her pussy muscles, and Sawyer groaned. It was the first chink in his armor she'd seen all night, the first time he'd let his own raging desires surface. Where her constant struggle to remain in power wore her out, Sawyer embraced his need for supremacy. It defined him, made him the wonderful lover he was.

His fingers tangled in her hair, and he pressed his lips against hers in a hard, demanding kiss. His hips continued to move as his cock filled her. "Come, Leah."

His voice was deep, commanding. He wouldn't settle for defeat, and he wouldn't let her get away with faking it. It didn't matter. Neither were options for her. He moved faster, and her head flew back against the pillow as an unfamiliar sensation rumbled through her. Her pussy clamped down once more, harder this time, and it held. She screamed, her fingers gripping the straps at her wrists, needing something to hold her to the planet. She was flying apart. Bright, white lights flashed behind her closed eyelids as sharp pricks of lightning struck her.

Sawyer held still throughout her orgasm and when she finally found the strength to open her eyes, his gaze was on her face.

"Jesus. That was incredible," he murmured.

She cried out, her body shuddering when he pulled out. "Wait...you didn't—"

He flipped her as if she weighed no more than a rag doll, the ties on her wrists twisting easily. She was certainly boneless enough to play that part.

"Let me worry about myself, Leah. Do that again." He lifted her hips and drilled to the hilt from behind. Within three thrusts, she was facing the pinnacle once more. His hand wrapped around her waist, pressing firmly against her clit, rubbing it until her toes tingled.

"Again, God dammit." His harsh command was all she needed as she plunged from the cliff into the abyss. She trembled, biting the pillow beneath her as the earth-shaking spasms racked her body. It was too much. It wasn't enough. She'd never get enough of Sawyer, of this.

Exhaustion claimed her as she fell face-first into the pillow, gasping for breath, but Sawyer offered her no surcease.

He pulled out again and turned her to her back. She whimpered at the movement, her body ultra-sensitive to every touch.

"Together," he whispered as he slowly reentered her quivering cunt. Leah gave herself up to his warm embrace.

He rocked inside her almost gently. She was overwhelmed by the care behind his actions. He kissed her, slowly showing her exactly how much he had to offer. While he would rock her world with the pain, the intensity, the forbidden, he could also take her to the same plateau with soft touches and tender kisses.

The crush she'd harbored for Sawyer for years made the transformation into something deeper and infinitely more dangerous.

She was falling for Sawyer Compton.

That realization jarred her harder than any wicked demand Sawyer might make, and her climax blossomed. The impact was softer, but no less powerful. She shuddered, refusing to close her eyes. Sawyer was with her, and she studied his face as he let go of his own hard-earned control.

She wasn't disappointed when his eyes drifted shut and his strong body trembled. A long stream of babbling fell from his lips as his hips jarred against hers of their own volition.

"Jesus. Leah. So. Fucking. Good. My rose."

She wrapped herself up in his praise and committed his face—in this moment—to memory. She suspected she wouldn't have any trouble bringing herself to orgasm with her vibrator when she returned home alone. She'd only have to close her eyes and imagine Sawyer's handsome face, his powerful voice and she'd be there.

She'd had an orgasm. She'd done it. Leah struggled to wrap her head around the realization, the relief that she'd finally been able to come. She'd honestly believed she was broken. Sawyer had set that fear to rest with his patience and his skill. Unlike past lovers, he hadn't written her off, assuming since her needs couldn't be met, he didn't need to make the attempt. He'd given her a wonderful gift.

He'd broken down a barrier inside her tonight, and he was well on his way to demolishing a few more. She should try to regain some sort of foothold, but she couldn't summon the energy to make the attempt.

She was too content in the here and now. She'd worry about the rest once the party was over.

Sawyer untied her hands. She tugged them down, trying to hide her wince of pain. She shouldn't have wasted the effort. Sawyer was too attuned to her reactions.

"Roll over." As always, he had her halfway to the position he demanded before she had a chance to respond.

She groaned when he straddled her thighs and started massaging her neck and shoulders.

"Oh my God. That's so good."

"I shouldn't have kept you tied up for so long. Didn't realize you were going to be such a hard nut to crack."

She laughed. "Yeah, that's me. Tough as leather."

He bent down and placed a soft kiss on her hair. "I think you pretend to be tough on the outside, but I know better. Inside you're pure marshmallow."

"Damn. And here I was, thinking I had everyone fooled."

He crawled to her side, claiming more than his fair share of the mattress. It didn't matter when he lifted her slightly until her head rested on his chest, his muscular arms engulfing her in his hold.

He squeezed her lightly. "Not me."

She giggled lightly. "I can't believe we're here like this."

"I don't think it's that far out of the realm of believability. Not sure Sam would be too surprised by it."

"Maybe not Sam, but Beth and her vicious pack would definitely keel over."

"Beth might have been an airhead, but I never really saw her as a bitch."

"That's because you're a guy. She made no secret of the fact she didn't like that you and I were friends."

Sawyer tipped her face up until she was looking at him. "I didn't know she was mean to you."

She shrugged. "Oh, it wasn't anything serious. She made fun of my clothes and hair. Typical girl stuff." While she'd been careful to hide from Sawyer exactly how poor she and her mother had been, it hadn't been that hard for the other girls to recognize the old clothes they'd donated to charity being worn by a classmate or the fact she clumsily trimmed her own hair.

"Is that why you hung out with me and Sam instead? I always assumed you found girls annoying and steered clear of them. I know I did."

"You avoided them? Wow. I missed that part. From where I stood, it looked like you constantly had a pack of them following you around like groupies."

Sawyer winked at her. "Damn. You're making me miss high school."

"Well, I don't. Not at all."

"I didn't realize how hard it was for you. Why didn't you say anything?"

"It was no big deal."

He placed his finger against her lips before she could continue spewing the same lies she'd relied on a million times before. It had hurt when classmates made fun of her, but she'd had to pretend, had to don a blasé look or be crushed by the humiliation.

"Don't. Don't ever lie to me. You can spout that bullshit to the world if it makes it easier for you, but don't do that with me."

She hadn't expected the tears his kind comment provoked. She wasn't a crier by nature, and she couldn't understand why Sawyer being nice to her would trigger the emotion after years of teasing hadn't.

"It was high school, Sawyer. A lifetime ago." She smiled as she spoke. She was an adult and the things that had tormented her when she was younger didn't carry the same importance.

He placed a soft kiss on her forehead. "I don't like the idea of anyone hurting you."

She lifted her head and gave him an amused grin. "Is that so?"

He caught her meaning and laughed. "I should say anyone who isn't me. And to clarify the difference, you seemed to enjoy the pain I was giving you." His face sobered. "You never said the safe words. Are you sure you didn't need to?"

She looked down at her hand as she ran it along his smooth chest. His body looked like it was chiseled in stone.

"I loved every minute of what we did together."

He cupped her face, forced her gaze to his. "So did I. We're not finished here, Leah. There are a million things I'm going to do with you."

A rush of warmth accompanied his words until reality came knocking on the door. "Sounds like it's going to be a busy weekend."

He started to speak, but talking about the end of this adventure made her stomach ache. Not yet. She silenced him with a quick kiss. For now, they had another whole day ahead of them and she refused to waste a minute of it worrying about what came after.

"Guess that means I won't have a chance to sneak in a trip to the beach."

"The beach?"

She shrugged. "I didn't realize this party would last more than one night until I got to Stacey's. My flight leaves fairly early on Sunday and I was really hoping there would be time for me to see the ocean. I've always wondered what it looks like."

Sawyer's eyes widened in shock. "You've never seen it?"

"I grew up in Wyoming, Saw. My mom and I barely had enough money for groceries, let alone for some trip to the sea."

"What about college? Spring break?"

She rolled her eyes. "I worked every holiday and summer to afford tuition."

"I'm taking you tomorrow."

"Is that allowed?"

It was Sawyer's turn to roll his eyes. "We're not freaking captives here, Leah. It's a party. We can come and go as we please."

She put her head on his chest and smiled. "I'd love to go see the ocean with you. Thanks."

He tightened his grip and his breathing slowed as sleep came to take them both away.

"Good night, rose."

"Good night, Sawyer."

Chapter Four

Sawyer took Leah's hand while trying to get a handle on the emotions rumbling around inside him. They meandered along the shore in silence, watching the people pass while enjoying the scenery.

He took a deep breath of the sea air and sighed. Leah had thrown him for a loop. Last night, his true feelings for her had come to the forefront when he realized she was wandering around the party as an unattached submissive. The idea of another man claiming what he'd always wanted had him seeing red. He didn't like to think about what would have happened if he'd arrived at the party too late—if Leah had accepted another man's invitation. He didn't doubt he would have made a scene and broken every rule of the house to steal that claim away.

After spending an entire evening with her tied to his bed, he'd realized Leah offered the best of both worlds—a sub in the bedroom and a partner everywhere else. She reminded him in a lot of ways of his mother, Vicky. Both women were spirited, beautiful, opinionated, loving.

Something JD had told him once drifted back to him. Sawyer had come home for Christmas three years after he'd joined the Coast Guard. His mom and dad had put decorations on the tree, retelling the memories attached to each ornament. None of his other brothers had been able to make the trip, so he'd had his parents to himself that year—a rarity.

Every now and then, JD would steal a kiss or lightly pinch his mom's ass, making her giggle, and Sawyer teased them about being worse than a couple of teenagers. JD had told him, "Sawyer, when the Compton men fall, they fall hard and forever. Might take you awhile to find the one, but when you do, it'll hit you in the face like a brick."

Sawyer had first felt the sting of that blow when they were eight years old and as they grew older, the stirrings definitely remained. For years, he had pushed them away for a million little reasons that failed to make sense to him now.

Sawyer rubbed his jaw as he looked at Leah and grinned. He halfway expected to discover a big knot from the cinderblock that had finally taken him down last night. When JD was right, he was right.

Leah kicked off her shoes, tossing them in the sand, wiggling her toes and laughing. She seemed so different from the serious girl she used to be. He'd noticed with each progressive trip home that she was changing, evolving. She was more comfortable in her own skin these days. She was happier, more at ease, freer.

He recalled her comments about high school and marveled at how differently they'd viewed that time. Leah claimed she'd been putting on a tough front, and he had to admit, she'd fooled him. Sawyer always marveled at how poised she was as a teenager. She seemed to possess the things most girls her age didn't. Self-confidence, maturity, intelligence. From his perspective, she'd never bought into the high school scene or its games. She didn't care what clothes were in style, didn't bother with makeup, didn't try to finagle invitations to the popular kids' parties. She'd always stood out to him as something special, something different.

She smiled at him. "Wow. I can't believe how beautiful the ocean is."

Sawyer was still reeling from Leah's admission that she'd

never seen it before. Of course, he shouldn't have been surprised. She'd gone straight home to Compton Pass after graduating from college. Leah was too careful with her money to indulge in a frivolous vacation, and the fact she'd saved for this trip drove home how very bad her sex life must have been.

She lifted her arms to soak in the sun and the fresh sea air. Her actions reminded him of the first time he'd seen the ocean. There was something so majestic, so breathtaking about it. Even after years with the Coast Guard and working around the water, he never ceased to be amazed by the power of it.

Though lately, he'd found himself missing the land. He longed to see the mountains, feel the crisp, cool breeze in his face as he rode his horse over fields so green they sometimes made him wonder if he'd taken a trip to Oz. Leah reminded him of home and family. Things he'd merely tolerated while growing up—barn dances, neighborhood picnics, ranch chores— suddenly had him yearning to return to Wyoming.

Leah squealed as a cold wave crashed around her bare feet. The sea breeze lifted her auburn hair, blowing it around her porcelain face. He used to stare at her in gym class, wondering why all the other guys seemed oblivious to the hottest girl in school.

It was a gorgeous day. The sun was shining brightly with enough wind to keep them from getting too hot. Sawyer yanked his T-shirt over his head, dropping it in the sand behind them where they'd left their shoes.

Leah's gasp had him spinning toward her.

"Leah?"

"Your tattoo. Turn around."

She hadn't seen it yet. He'd risen before her this morning, throwing on his clothes and venturing downstairs to find them coffee and breakfast. After that, they'd made out like teenagers for nearly an hour before he told her to get dressed for their outing. He hadn't pressed for more sex, afraid she might be too sore from the previous night.

He angled his back toward her, curious about her response.

"Wow. That's incredible. Who did it?"

"Snake."

Her fingers traced the ink on his skin. "I figured it had to be someone from home. It's so realistic."

"My brothers have the same one."

"All of them?"

He nodded. "Each of us has small variations. On mine, the W is larger than the other compass points. The Pacific Ocean has been calling me since I was a kid. Seth opted for a bigger S, Sam has a fancy E and Silas started it all with a big honking N on his back."

She continued caressing his back. "The tattoo as a whole is impressive, but it's the details that are really amazing. Is there significance to all of it?"

"Yeah. Most of it is there for a reason. The ranch and brand obviously represent home, the smaller compass points are there for my brothers. I had Snake ink in a JD and a V for my parents. They're intertwined there in the center of the compass. See them?"

She touched the spot, her voice sounding a bit choked up. "That's so sweet."

He chuckled. "Christ, rose. Don't say that too loud. I got the tattoo to look tough."

She placed a soft kiss on his tattoo and he closed his eyes, wondering how such a simple gesture could pierce his heart like an arrow. "You know what I mean."

He was confused by the comment and the sudden sadness in her tone, but he dismissed it when her fingers began tracing the pattern again. "I like this the best."

"Which part?"

Her finger drew a W on his back. He understood what had caught her interest. "The way Snake designed the W. Is it made up of dandelions?"

He swallowed heavily. "Yeah."

He shifted before she could look too closely at the rest of the tattoo. He wasn't ready for her to study all the details. If so, she'd realize there was a rose growing out of the ranch brand. That part of the tattoo had been added at the last minute—a silly whim he thought he'd regret later. As the years passed, the rose continued to be his favorite part of the whole tat.

He kissed her, cutting off any more conversation about his tattoo. She welcomed his embrace, wrapping her hands around his waist.

He pulled away. "I'm glad you like it. It's pretty big. More than a few women turn their nose up at it."

"I think it's the sexiest thing I've ever seen."

He grinned and kissed her again, a short, hard press of his lips against hers. Then he twisted her until they faced the ocean together, enveloping her in his arms.

They were silent for several minutes as they studied the white caps and listened to the mighty roar of the sea.

"I can see why you've chosen this life, Sawyer. There's something very hypnotic about it all, isn't there? The constant, soothing rhythm of the waves, the endless horizon, the gentle way the water and sand work together to massage your feet. It's incredible."

He nodded. It was, but it wasn't enough.

"I'm leaving the Coast Guard." He wasn't sure why he'd blurted it out like that. Though his decision had been ninety-five percent made, he hadn't taken that final leap to say aloud, *I'm going home,* to anyone.

Leah took his hand in hers, giving him a sad smile. "I'm not surprised. I mean all your other brothers have done the same. I'm really sorry about your dad, Sawyer."

Her comment caught him off-guard. "JD?"

Leah tilted her head, confused. "About his cancer. I can't imagine Compton Pass without him."

Sawyer stared at her, trying to process what she was saying. *Cancer? JD?* "What the fuck are you talking about?"

He hadn't meant to sound so harsh, so angry, but pieces fell together, adding up to something he simply couldn't—wouldn't—believe.

Leah paled, dropping his hand. "Oh God. I'm sorry. I thought you knew."

"Knew what?"

She bit her lip, shaking her head slightly. "I shouldn't be the one to say—"

"God dammit, Leah. Tell me."

Tears formed in her eyes, and he briefly wondered if he'd frightened her. When she spoke again, he understood what was driving the tears. "JD has pancreatic cancer. He's dying."

"No." He shook his head. "That's not possible. There's no way Sam would have kept that from me. You must've heard wrong."

Leah didn't respond. Clearly she wouldn't criticize his brother for doing exactly that. Sawyer recalled Sam's phone call last night. There'd been something in his voice. He'd thought there was a complication with Silas. Now...

"How long have you known?"

She shrugged. "I don't know. Maybe a month. Or actually, more than that."

Sawyer's head exploded. "Are you kidding me?" He ran his hand through his hair, trying to understand. He pulled his cell out of his pocket. "I need to call Sam."

Leah nodded, but didn't say more.

Sawyer clenched his fist when he heard his brother's casual answer. "Hey bro."

"Sam." He didn't bother to hide the coldness in his tone. If Leah were telling the truth...

"What's up, man? Didn't expect to hear from you this early. Not since you were so busy."

"Yeah, that's me. The brother too fucking busy to come back to Wyoming."

There was a brief moment of silence on the other end before Sam tried to take cover from the torpedo about to blow his ass out of the water. "Sawyer, I can explain—"

"Tell you what," Sawyer interrupted. "Why don't you start with the part where you tell me what the fuck is going on with JD?"

Sam sucked in a deep breath for what was coming next. "Sounds like you already know."

"I want to hear it from you. The person who should've told me to begin with."

"JD forbade us to say anything to you."

The overpowering need to hit something churned in his gut. Where was a sturdy oak when you needed one? He bet he could break every bone in his hand and still not feel the pain over the one growing in his chest.

"And being the good little son, you did exactly what your

daddy told you to do. Say the fucking words, Sam."

"It's cancer. JD's dying."

Sawyer doubled over. He put his hand on his knee as he fought a wave of nausea.

"I'm sorry, Sawyer."

Sawyer's vision went red. He didn't need his brother's fucking pity. He'd needed the truth. He forced himself to stand upright, took a deep breath and struggled to hang on. He could do this. "I'm coming home. Tonight if I can swing it. If not, on the first available flight."

"I'll pick you up at the airport," Sam offered.

Sawyer glanced at Leah—her face rife with anguish. "No. I have a ride. I don't need any favors from you."

"God dammit, Sawyer, you've got to let me explain—"

Sawyer exploded. The time for discussion had long since passed. "When I get there, I'm kicking your ass. Explain it to my knuckles. Might take a piece out of Silas's and Seth's hides for good measure. Share that message with them, will you?"

He clicked the phone off before Sam could reply. He'd heard all he could stand from his twin, uncertain which hurt worse— his father's cancer or his brother's betrayal.

He stared at the waves and dragged air into his lungs. The ocean, which had sounded so loud earlier, was nothing but a quiet din in the distance compared to the sound of his heart pounding mercilessly loud and fast. He wasn't sure he'd ever experienced true terror until this moment.

Leah gently touched his arm. "Sawyer?"

He cleared his throat, unable to face her. Part of him yearned to fall into her arms and cry like a fucking baby. He wouldn't do that. He sucked in another deep breath. Fought for control.

"I need to go home."

"I know."

When his raging emotions were locked away once more, he looked at her. "JD's dying. They didn't tell me."

"Did Sam give you a reason?"

He shook his head. "Not a good one. All my brothers are home?"

She nodded. "Sam came home a couple months ago. Right after Seth moved back. You didn't know that? When's the last time you spoke to your family?"

He considered the question, trying to remember. "I've been at sea for the past eight weeks. I was out of contact a lot and then I dropped my last damn cell phone overboard." It didn't matter. None of that was relevant. His brothers had had plenty of opportunities and ways to reach him. They simply hadn't.

The shock and pain at JD's diagnosis gave way to rage so bone-deep it almost shattered him. Sawyer welcomed it. Anger he could channel, use to his benefit. He might be helpless in the face of his father's illness, but by God, he wasn't some weak-minded boy. His brothers had always considered him the baby of the family. They were about to get a rude awakening to exactly how much of a man he'd grown up to be.

His fists clenched as he plotted retribution. He was going to kick every single one of their asses from Wyoming to Kansas.

Leah wrapped her hands around one of his, trying to loosen the tight grip. "Give them a chance to explain, Saw. You're angry and hurt, but violence isn't going to change what's happened."

She was wrong. Violence was exactly what he needed.

Chapter Five

They reentered the bedroom they'd left only a few hours earlier. Dead silence. Sawyer closed the door, *snicking* the lock into place. Pain was etched in every line on his face and Leah ached to take some of it away. He'd managed to snag the last seat on the same flight home as her, but it wouldn't leave until morning. Waiting one more night was going to be hard for him.

"Sawyer—"

He raised his hand, halting her attempt to talk. "I need—" He was breathing rapidly, his eyes dark with anguish. He paused as if fighting with himself.

He didn't say more. He didn't have to.

She knelt slowly before him, the action visibly jarring him. Her gaze never left his face as she assumed the submissive pose. "I know what you need."

He reared away, pressing his shoulders against the door. For a moment, she thought he might unlock it and run.

"I can't be gentle." His warning confirmed her suspicions. He'd held back. He hadn't been honest about his own desires.

That thought touched and infuriated her simultaneously. It was so typically Sawyer to try to shelter her. Even when she didn't need his protection.

"Last night, you said the only thing that would anger you was if I hid my feelings."

His eyes narrowed suspiciously. "Did you?"

"No. You did, though."

He started to deny her assertion, but she cut him off.

"You wanted more from me, Sawyer, but you didn't take it. You acted like last night was enough."

"It was."

She shook her head. "I don't believe you."

His chest rose and fell rapidly. She wondered if she was wrong to taunt him, then she decided he might welcome a distraction, something to take his mind off the tragedy awaiting him at home. It was clear he'd been devastated by what he viewed as his brothers' betrayal. Her Sawyer was a man who prided himself on being strong, in command of his own destiny. His brothers had taken that power away, stripped away his right to decide what was best for him.

"I don't regret a single minute of last night, Leah. You're new to this lifestyle. I had to take it slow."

She flung her hair over her shoulder. "Stop treating me like some weak little girl who can't take care of herself. If you don't think I can be what you need, maybe I should find someone else."

She started to rise, but he halted her, his strong hands pressing on her shoulders. "Don't test me on this, Leah. Now isn't the time—"

"Give me the white wristband back. I want the chance to find a Dom who isn't afraid to take off the kid gloves. I told you last night, Sawyer. We have too much history. This just proves my point."

Sawyer gripped her hair tightly in his fists. "You aren't going anywhere."

"I'm not staying." She was trying to provoke him, but her threats were working some sort of magic on her as well. Last night, they'd only scratched the surface of her desire for pain and dominance.

She wasn't certain they'd ever break through this barrier unless she prodded. Her pussy grew wetter, hotter as she imagined exactly how much more she could take from him. "I need more."

His fingers loosened, and she could tell she'd shocked him. She broke free of his grip and rose, stepping away before he could grab her.

"God dammit, Leah. I won't let you leave. You're mine."

"Ha!" She darted to the left, putting the bed between them as a barrier. Her heart raced when he took a step closer, his stance firm, menacing, sexy as hell. "I'm not that easy."

Sawyer put his hands on his hips. She rejoiced when the pain that had ravaged his face all day faded, replaced by determination. Her powerful man was returning. Maybe he didn't have control over what was happening in his family, but she could give him this chance to take charge, to find his bearings for a little while.

God, she wished she were so benevolent. Truth was she was a selfish bitch, and she was forcing his hand for her own greedy purposes.

"Don't make me chase you, rose. I warned you last night about saying no to me."

She shrugged nonchalantly. "You'd have to catch me first." She taunted him, beckoning him with her finger. "Come and get it. If you think you're man enough."

He reacted like a sprinter to the starting pistol. She'd expected him to go around the bed, so she was caught off guard when he lunged over the king-sized mattress. She bolted to her right in an attempt to escape. Sawyer anticipated her direction, charging after her. His fingertips brushed her arm, but while he was forced to find his balance on the mattress, she was on firm ground.

She dashed to the door, struggling with the lock. If he'd failed to engage it, she would have made it to the hall. Instead, the few seconds it took were seconds she didn't have. Sawyer pressed her against the door, trapping her with his body before she could open it.

His lips touched her ear, and he practically growled at her through gritted teeth. "What are your safe words?"

She shook her head. She wasn't quitting.

"Let me hear the words, Leah."

"Fuck you."

He bit her earlobe—hard. "Fucking say them."

She tried to shove him away, then threw an elbow into his gut. He grunted, but didn't move.

"You're going to pay for that."

She snorted. "Empty threat. I'd like to see you try to back it up."

He reached for her hands and she struggled. She wouldn't make this easy for him.

As she batted him away—her nipples tight, her pussy on fire—she realized she *needed* to battle him. She wanted him to force her. It was the only way her mind would accept his domination.

"Last chance, Leah. Safe words. I can't promise..."

His warning drifted into nothing. Rather than reply, she lifted her leg and stomped on his foot with all the power she could muster. His surprise gave her the time she needed, and she escaped his hold. She'd only managed to take a few steps toward the bed when Sawyer tackled her from behind. His momentum propelled her facedown on the mattress.

She tried to regain her freedom, but Sawyer had the

advantage of size and strength. His entire body covered hers, leaving her powerless.

"You're mine," he said again.

Her heart rejoiced at the declaration even if her ever-practical mind screamed a reminder that this was only a short-term deal.

She might not be able to physically resist him, but she wasn't finished fighting yet. "No," she taunted. "I'm not."

His body tensed. When he went for her hands again, he captured them with ease. He pulled them behind her back roughly, retaining his grip on them with one of his. With his other hand, he lifted himself away from the bed, dragging her along with him.

He might not accept the word no, but she didn't doubt for a moment, he'd release her the instant she uttered one of her safe words. She'd never felt so exhilarated, wondering how it was possible to experience so many emotions at once—fear, excitement, desire.

He led her to the wooden structure she'd noticed secured to the wall the night before. So much had happened between them, and yet she hadn't had a chance to ask him about all the odd furnishings. They didn't stop moving until she was face-to-face with the large, rather-threatening-looking frame.

"X marks the spot?" she asked.

"It's a St. Andrew's Cross." That was the only explanation he gave as he twisted her, pressing her against the leather pads, strapping first one and then the other hand to the structure. Her head rested against the wall on which the cross was affixed.

"Shoes," he commanded.

Leah didn't need further explanation as she toed off her

sandals. Sawyer's hands appeared at her waist as he removed her shorts and panties. His hands lightly caressed her hips and thighs as he knelt before her.

Taking her ankle in his hand, he pulled until he could secure it to one foot of the structure. Leah shuddered. While she'd enjoyed Sawyer's bondage last night in bed, there was something so much more exciting about being bound against the beams. Last night's capture had seemed intimate while this couldn't be misconstrued as anything less than true imprisonment, helplessness.

Sawyer hooked her other ankle to the last leg of the cross and stepped away. She was spread-eagle against the wall, the chains at her feet and wrists allowing her no opportunity for movement.

"Do you love this shirt?"

Leah noticed the scissors he picked up from the desk. She shook her head. Without another word, he cut the T-shirt and bra off her body, rendering her completely naked.

She was breathless with anticipation. A drop of arousal trickled down her inner thigh. This was the single hottest moment of her life.

Sawyer ran his hand along her stomach. She shivered at the gentle touch—a direct contrast to the wicked hold of his straps. He dragged his fingers along her slit.

"So wet," he whispered.

"Please," she groaned when he pulled them away. She needed to be touched, taken, anything.

"You were a naughty girl, Leah. You have to be punished."

"Yes," she hissed.

He placed a kiss on her forehead, and she sensed his conflict. He couldn't separate the Leah he'd known from the woman she'd become. He'd always viewed her as someone he needed to protect.

"You aren't allowed to come until I say so."

She nodded. She remembered that rule.

He gave her a wicked grin. "I'm not going to give you permission."

She frowned. "What?"

"I'm going to play with you until you have no choice but to come. Then I'm going discipline you for disobeying."

He glanced around the room, his gaze landing on the leather bench near the bed. She imagined a repeat of last night's amazing spanking.

She wished what he described didn't sound so damned appealing. She was having a hard time thinking of anything Sawyer did to her as punishment. "Isn't that cheating?"

He shrugged. "Maybe. Do you want it?"

"God, yes."

He chuckled. "I can't really punish you, Leah. I know what you're doing."

Her heart lurched painfully. "You do?"

"You're distracting me. Giving me a chance to be in control." He placed his forehead against hers. "You're saving me."

She blinked rapidly, refusing to mar this moment with tears. Instead, she threw out a taunt. "You know, I've never noticed how much you run your mouth. Any chance I can get you to shut up now? Less talk, more action?"

He raised his eyebrow and pinched her nipple roughly. "Watch it, Leah."

She gasped when he increased the pressure on the tight

nub. Her head fell against the wall, and she groaned. "Mmm. Where did you put those nipple clamps?"

Sawyer didn't respond. Instead, he applied the same pressure to her other breast. "Topping from the bottom again. Bad girl."

She paid for her wayward tongue, as Sawyer promised she would. He took the meaning of self-restraint to an entirely new level as he tormented every inch of her body. He covered her with little bits of pain—a bite on her breast, a pinch on her thigh. Then he'd kiss each tiny hurt better with his lips. After nearly a half an hour of teasing her breasts, he finally gave her the clamps she'd requested. This pair was different from the ones the night before, the tension stronger.

Leah groaned when he placed them on her nipples. Bolts of arousal weakened her resistance to come. He'd told her not to. Leah's pride wouldn't let her give in easily. She resisted her climax, pushing it away until she was physically wrung out.

Her body was on fire, but he'd sealed her fate when he'd told her she'd lose. He'd known what he was doing. He'd piqued her stubbornness, and now she was paying for the character flaw.

She clenched her fists and forced herself not to look down, as Sawyer knelt between her legs, sucking on her clit like his life depended on it. Her entire body trembled as she tried to defy her orgasm. When he drove two fingers into her pussy, it was a lost cause.

"Please," she cried. "Please fuck me. Let me come."

He placed a light kiss on her thigh. "No."

"Dammit, Sawyer. You're killing me."

He chuckled, his hot breath tickling her sensitive pussy. Her toes clenched and she wrestled against the chains holding her defenseless against his sensual torment, reeling at the irony of her situation. Last night, she'd struggled to come, thinking that sexual reward beyond her grasp.

Oh how the tide had turned.

Sawyer's mouth returned to her clit at the same time he shoved one wet finger into her ass. She disintegrated. She crumbled. She came.

Sawyer pressed his forehead to her stomach as she rode out the storm.

Gasping, sweaty, she hung bonelessly from the beams. Sawyer slowly began unhooking her ankles. He made sure she'd found her feet before releasing her wrists. Once she was completely free, he was there to catch her, to support her.

He shook his head, as if disappointed in her. "Naughty girl."

She didn't have the strength to laugh. "Sorry." Her tone betrayed her lack of remorse.

Sawyer leaned her against the cross, keeping a firm hand on her shoulder to ensure she stayed upright. She wasn't *that* weak, but before she could speak, he removed one of the nipple clamps.

Pain and arousal streaked through her like wildfire, and she was suddenly grateful for Sawyer's supportive hold as another climax rumbled through her body. She was only a bit more prepared when he removed the second clamp. Tossing them to the floor, he stepped closer, caging her to the wall with his body as his lips descended to offer sweet relief to her sore nipples.

"How can I love something so much when it hurts like shit?"

Sawyer looked at her, his face such an odd mixture of emotions she wasn't sure what she was seeing. "You're incredible, Leah."

She smiled at the compliment. "I'm a freak."

He laughed. "If that's true then I'm a lunatic because I love exploring your limits and your tolerance for pain. Love watching you explode. A man could get addicted to you."

She didn't care about other men, but she wouldn't mind having Sawyer captivated by her. At least then she wouldn't feel so alone in her overwhelming infatuation.

He held her for a few moments, the two of them simply standing in each other's arms. She tried to soak up as much of his strength as possible. She recalled his earlier threat and realized they were only in the early stages of this game.

Sawyer cupped her face with his hand. "Ready to try the bench?"

She nodded. "Very."

He kissed her softly, before murmuring, "Addicted."

He led her to the apparatus, giving her a chance to study the shape.

"Kneel."

She placed her knees on the cushion. Sawyer pressed on her shoulders, splaying her over the angled top until her head was slightly lower than her ass.

She started when he gripped her ankles and secured them to the sides of the bench. Once again, he'd found a new way to leave her exposed. She wasn't sure what it said about her that she craved this type of bondage.

"I'm not going to tie your hands this time. Put them down and grip the base."

She obeyed as a second wind came over her. Sheer giddy excitement wiped away her previous exhaustion. She fidgeted, anxiously awaiting his spanking. She'd loved the heat and pain he'd produced last night. Her pussy clenched, hungrily.

"Hurry," she pleaded.

Sawyer sighed. "You need to stop trying to run the show, Leah. Maybe you need a stronger reminder of who's in control here."

She lifted her head and started to look over her shoulder at him, but he halted her.

"Eyes forward or I'll blindfold you again."

She turned her head to the front, facing the wall before her. It was then she realized there was a mirror hanging directly before them.

Sawyer winked at her in the reflection. "This way I can see all of you—your pretty face, your red ass. And you can see..." He reached behind him for something. When he raised his hand, she spotted the paddle.

Her breath caught, but she was careful not to reveal too much. Sawyer studied her expression, looking for any reaction that would give him a reason to stop.

Her arousal grew at the idea of Sawyer paddling her bare bottom. She must've failed in her attempt to hide her desire.

Sawyer didn't give her time to wonder about the sensation. After his standard pause for the safe word, he lifted it and swung. Leah groaned, the impact so different from his hand. Because the paddle covered a larger area, it actually didn't hurt as much as Sawyer's palm. Or so she thought until his next swing.

"God," she yelled, her ass stinging.

Sawyer planted several more slaps before he dropped it, running his fingers along her slit.

She cried out with relief when he drove two fingers into her pussy roughly. He increased the pace gradually until Leah's vision dimmed with light-headedness.

"Have to come. Have to come," she panted out the constant mantra.

"No. You're not allowed."

"Please. God, please," she yelled. This game was too much, too good.

He added two more smacks on her sore bottom with his hand and another finger to the pair in her pussy, currently driving her insane.

"I can't stop," she said, before screaming as her orgasm crashed in on her. She retained a death grip on the base of the bench, pushing her hips against his fingers, wishing it was his cock inside her. She pressed her forehead against the leather beneath her as she tried to recover from the powerful climax.

Sawyer's hands in her hair brought her to her senses. When had he moved? She lifted her head and found him kneeling in front of her. Somewhere along the line he'd shed his clothing and his hard cock was inches from her face. He really had left her senseless.

She grinned and reached for him.

Sawyer grasped her hands before she could claim her prize and shook his head. "Leave them where they were. You aren't allowed to touch me."

She started to protest, but Sawyer raised a single eyebrow. "Ready for another spanking so soon?"

She closed her mouth.

"Who controls your body?"

She licked her lips. "You do." The answer came much easier tonight. There was no point in denying something that was so obvious to both of them.

"There's a difference between a blowjob and what I'm about

to do."

"Okay."

He grinned at her worried tone. "Don't look so nervous. You'll like this. I want to fuck your mouth. Open up."

She parted her lips, realizing how easy it was for her to follow Sawyer's commands. He asked for something, and she didn't hesitate to give it to him. Eventually she'd need time to understand what that meant, but it wasn't going to happen now.

The moment her mouth fell open, Sawyer was there, the head of his cock rubbing against her lips. She tried to capture the drops of pre-come, but he shook his head when she touched him with her tongue.

"No, Leah. This isn't a blowjob. I'm fucking you. Open your mouth and hold on."

That was the only warning she got before his cock dove deeper into her mouth. She felt compelled to participate—suck, lick, something—but every time she started to get involved, Sawyer pulled away.

After his third retreat, he cupped her face and raised her gaze to his. "What part of *just* open your mouth is giving you trouble?"

She narrowed her eyes at his smartass question, ready to eviscerate him. "Sawyer. I'm trying—"

"No. You aren't. I understand that you have issues with needing to be in charge and I wasn't foolish enough to think that you'd overcome them all last night, regardless of how sweetly you submitted to me. But this exploration isn't going to end tomorrow. We're returning to Compton Pass together."

She licked her lips uncomfortably. "We're sharing a flight. Of course, we're going home together."

"That's not what I mean and you know it."

She shook her head. "Maybe you should spell it out."

"I can't let this end yet."

"This?" She needed him to explain exactly what it was he expected from her. She knew all too well what she hoped for, but she didn't think that was what he was saying. Besides, while she'd had several orgasms in the past hour or so, Sawyer had yet to give in once. Was this his cock talking or his brain?

"We've only scratched the surface of all the things I can show you. You aren't dating anyone at home, right?"

She shook her head. "No, I'm not seeing anyone right now."

"I think we should continue exploring your limits."

He wanted to keep playing BDSM games with her? He made no mention of dating, of pursuing a relationship. She was torn. While she wanted what he was offering, she wasn't sure she could keep her heart from hoping for more, something he didn't sound willing to offer.

"But your family—"

"Is fucked up right now. I'm not saying it's going to be easy, but I know I can't survive what comes next without this."

She was speechless. Every word he said chiseled itself into her heart. He wanted more time with her. He needed the comfort she could offer. She was amazed, ecstatic, terrified.

"You don't have to answer now. Think about what I'm saying. I know it's sudden. We haven't seen each other much these past few years. I'm asking for your trust and a leap of faith, but I know when something is right, Leah, and this feels about as close to perfect as it gets."

She agreed. Their bodies and desires were made for each other. She couldn't debate that. If she were a different woman, she'd take exactly what he offered without a second's hesitation.

Unfortunately, she was afraid of what came after. What happened when he decided their explorations should end? Where would she be then?

"I don't know—"

Sawyer cut her off with a sexy grin. "You can argue and protest and all that bullshit, Leah, but I aim to get what I want and I don't plan on losing."

She laughed at his determination. "Wow. Way to offer me a choice."

He placed a soft kiss on the top of her head. "Oh, the decision is yours. I'm telling you to choose right," he teased.

She loved his humor.

"We'll talk about it later, rose. For now, open that sexy mouth."

This time, it was easier to obey. Sawyer pushed his cock inside as Leah's mind raced. He would keep her as his submissive lover. Could she do that? She'd warned him that her obedience began and ended at the bedroom door. Would he accept that while she might do his bidding in bed, she was an independent woman with a mind of her own? She made her own decisions, lived her life to suit her.

His hands tugged at her hair, and she groaned.

"I'm a selfish bastard when it comes to you, Leah."

She closed her eyes, reveling as his intimate possession drove her arousal higher. Regardless of her other concerns, her lust for Sawyer was far from burning out.

"I need you. Need this. You're so fucking sexy. Please, don't let this end tonight, rose."

She wondered if he was saying these things now because he felt safer talking to her when she couldn't answer. Could he truly fear she'd reject what he was offering? Did he think she'd deny him anything?

He'd told her to keep her hands on the bench, but she couldn't do it—couldn't listen to everything he was saying—without touching him. She gripped his waist. He paused briefly and she expected him to stop, to punish her. He did neither.

"I love your hands on me, your soft hair, your quiet cries. Jesus, Leah. I'm never going to get enough. I'll keep taking and taking because I can't resist you, your body, your orgasms. I'm going to claim your pussy, your ass, your mouth. They're mine now. I can't let you go."

She tightened her grip, tried to take him deeper. He wouldn't let her speak, so she'd have to show him without words. When his cock touched her throat again, she swallowed the head.

"Fuck," he grunted. "Shit. Can't stop."

He grasped her head more firmly as he moved into her mouth faster, deeper. The first drops of semen landed on her tongue, and she hummed her assent. The vibration was all Sawyer needed. Hot spurts of come painted the back of her throat. She swallowed as her fingers dug into his sweat-slicked waist, desperate to keep him close.

She protested lightly when he pulled out of her mouth, but her cries were cut off when he lifted her face and kissed her. His tongue tangled with hers. She wrapped her arms around his neck and held on for dear life as he deepened the embrace.

Eventually Sawyer rose. Leah clutched the leather bench, wonderfully exhausted. Sawyer untied her ankles and helped her to her feet. When she wobbled, he bent and picked her up, carrying her to bed as if she were a fragile China doll. He joined her on the mattress and resumed the kiss.

Soon their touches became more heated, his gentle caresses more urgent. When he climbed over her, she opened her legs and welcomed him in, wondering how she'd survived so many years without him.

He thrust into her and she was there to meet him halfway. They took their time, neither of them in a hurry to see the night end. Tomorrow would be here too soon and with it would come certain pain and heartache. For tonight, they could disappear into the darkness, into each other. Hopefully, they'd find enough strength in these moments to guide them through the days and weeks to come.

Chapter Six

Leah took the road that would lead Sawyer to his home more slowly than necessary. He knew what she was doing. All the stall tactics in the world weren't going to make a difference and they sure as shit weren't going to help him calm down. It had been a rather subdued trip to Wyoming. He'd said too much last night, trying to convince Leah to commit to a D/s affair. Even though it was the worst possible time to try to plan a future with someone, he'd panicked at the thought of ending their new relationship. Desperation had him firmly in its grip.

He'd lost so much yesterday—trust in his brothers, a long future with his father, a sense of home. He'd taken one look at Leah's sweet face and known he couldn't lose her too.

Of course, it would be a miracle if she didn't drop his ass off at the front door and run for the hills after his caveman-like *you're mine* speech.

He rubbed his forehead, trying to ward off the headache that had been threatening all morning. He hadn't managed more than a few hours of restless sleep last night as his mind raced over everything—Sam, JD, Leah, the Coast Guard resignation he'd faxed to his superior officer. His life was one giant powder keg sitting smack in the middle of a lightning storm. One strike and everything was going to be reduced to cinders.

He glanced at Leah. There were dark circles under her eyes that made him think she hadn't slept any better than him. They'd had to rush around this morning in order to make their flight. Once they'd boarded the plane, they were separated. His last-minute ticket purchase prevented them from snagging two seats together.

"Leah. About last night. I owe you an apology."

She frowned, but didn't take her eyes off the road. "What for?"

"I came on a little strong. I hope I didn't scare you."

Her hands tightened on the steering wheel and he bit back a curse. Shit. He really had frightened her.

She sighed. "It's okay. Yesterday was a pretty emotional day, Saw. I know better than to put too much stock in things said in the heat of the moment."

He looked at her. "I meant what I told you. We're going to keep going."

She glanced at him and for a second, he feared she'd refuse him.

Before she could answer, they turned on to the driveway of Compass ranch and Sawyer's stomach sunk.

"Fuck," he muttered.

Leah's gaze softened. "It'll all be okay. We can sort out our issues later. For now, you need to concentrate on your family."

Terror gripped him as he considered what was waiting for him at home. Leah had gently tried to prepare him for the changes the cancer had wrought in his tough-as-steel father. He prayed he'd be able to hold himself together.

Leah slowed the car more than the gravel driveway required. Her actions reminded him of Sam, and a cold calmness descended. The need to make someone hurt as much as he'd been aching since hearing about JD's illness inundated him. His deceitful brother would be a welcome punching bag.

"You might as well push on the gas pedal. The end result is

going to be the same whether it happens now or five minutes from now."

She glanced at him anxiously. "I think you need to take a deep breath and calm down. You're uptight."

He narrowed his eyes. "I'm perfectly relaxed. I'm going to have a little chat with my brothers. I don't give a good god damn if that's done verbally or with fists."

"Sawyer—"

"Don't, Leah. Don't try to placate me. They've been home for months. I should have been here too. JD is fucking dying. They had no right to deprive me of that time with my dad." He silently cursed as his voice cracked a bit. So many wasted days. It wasn't fair.

"I understand you're angry. Hell, I'd be pissed off too. I think you need to give them a chance to explain why they didn't call you."

"Do you honestly think there's any reason in the world that's fucking good enough to keep me from coming home?"

She winced as his yelling reverberated off the closed car windows. He leaned against the headrest and forced himself to inhale slowly. Maybe she was right. He needed to get a grip.

As they pulled up to the house, Sawyer turned to Leah.

She glanced at him warily. "I should head back to my apartment."

Sawyer shook his head. He was facing some of the hardest moments of his life. "No. Stay."

She started to argue, so he quickly added, "Please."

She released a long sigh. "I'd be in the way, Sawyer. This is your homecoming. It should just be family."

He disagreed. "I *need* you here. I can't do this alone, Leah."

She didn't answer. She simply reached for the handle and

opened the door, stepping out, giving him exactly what he asked for. God, he wasn't sure how he'd managed to find her at the exact moment he needed her most, but he was so grateful he had.

He followed suit, rounding the hood of the car, intent on grabbing her hand and leading her inside. He pulled up short when Sam moseyed down the path by the side of the house, grinning from ear to ear, with his arm wrapped around Cindi's shoulders. Great, Sawyer was in fucking agony, while his brother was fucking the ranch bookkeeper.

Sawyer saw red and changed direction.

Sam's smile wavered when he spotted Sawyer making a beeline for them like a nuclear torpedo.

In a few short steps, Sawyer was in front of his twin. Sam read his intentions, moving away from Cindi, taking her out of the line of fire.

Smart brother.

"Saw," his brother said, as his hands rose in surrender.

"You fucking prick." Sawyer didn't bother to say more. He simply clenched his fist and let it fly, punching his brother with more force than he'd ever used against another man in his life.

Sam staggered back a couple paces at the blow, but Sawyer had to hand it to his brother. He didn't fall or cower. Within seconds, Sam was moving forward, his own fists raised, ready to do battle. "If that's the way you're going to play, fucker. Fine. You're the asshole who won't listen."

Sawyer was waiting for him. He'd had too many hours to think of all the retribution his brother had coming to him. When Sam tried to reciprocate with a hard right, Sawyer was ready. He dodged the blow and followed up with a quick jab at Sam's stomach. He was about to throw another punch at his brother's face when a mass of red hair appeared between them.

101

Leah, the foolish woman, had thrown herself right smack dab in the middle of the brawl. Looking around, he noticed Cindi had done the same thing, saw her slim back as she shoved at Sam's chest, pushing him away.

Sawyer started after his brother, but Leah's hands landed on his shoulders.

"Stop!" she shouted.

He grasped her waist and lifted her out of his way with ease. "Dammit, Leah. You're going to get hurt." Sam had broken free of Cindi as well and was about to return to the brawl when a stronger hand landed on Sawyer's arm, keeping him from advancing on his twin.

Before he could shrug it off, he found himself spinning to face Seth. He grinned angrily. *Fuck it.* He didn't care which brother he pummeled. As far as he was concerned, Seth was as guilty as Sam.

He pushed Seth hard, the force of his action an invitation for more.

"God dammit," Seth yelled, his fists hanging by his sides. "You can't handle a piece of this, cub."

"I wouldn't be too sure of that."

"Sawyer, please." Leah tugged on the waistband of his jeans, but lost her grip when he twisted, his focus solely set on pummeling one or all of his brothers. From the corner of his eye, he saw Silas rushing from the barn, walking far too fast for his injured leg, his limp painfully pronounced despite the fact he was using his cane. Colby was trying to hold Sawyer's oldest brother back, but Silas wouldn't be deterred.

"Please, Sawyer," Leah said. "Stop this now before someone gets hurt."

"That's sort of my plan here, baby. Someone's gonna feel

some pain, and I don't give a shit who it is."

Seth took a step closer and Sawyer urged him on, taunting him. "Come on, brother. Take a swing if you think you're man enough."

"Don't you dare," a pretty brunette said from behind Seth before grabbing a handful of his brother's shirttail.

"He's asking for it, Jody," Seth said.

He could hear Sam arguing with Cindi and knew his brother was itching to get some of his own in the battle. Sawyer had connected with two solid blows, while Sam had yet to land one.

Sawyer stood in front of his family's house and glanced from Seth to Silas to Sam, wondering which man would make it to him first. Didn't matter who. Sawyer fully intended to be the last man standing in the brawl.

"Enough!"

All the arguing ceased at JD's deep command.

Sawyer froze, and then he forced himself to look toward the front porch where his father stood. All the air left his body in a pained whoosh when he saw the image of his larger-than-life dad shrunken with disease. A thousand punches from his brothers' hard knuckles wouldn't hurt as much as seeing his dad brought down by cancer. He'd gotten KO'd after all.

"Pa," he whispered. His throat closed up. His chest rose and fell heavily as he struggled to get a deep breath. Agony ripped through him like shards of glass, shredding everything in its path.

Before JD could reply, Vicky appeared at the front door. When she spotted him, she squealed with delight and raced down the steps to embrace him tightly. "Sawyer!"

Sawyer wrapped his arms around his mother, numb to her

hug as his gaze never left JD's face. There were deep lines, etched by pain, and his color seemed almost unnatural. His father's broad build had been reduced greatly and Sawyer suspected JD had lost at least forty pounds since the last time he'd been home.

Sawyer's insides were raw, his eyes gritty with unshed tears. He was equal parts anger and agony, unsure which end was up. He felt like he was dangling by his feet from a bridge, not sure whether to struggle to survive or to simply let go.

Vicky gave him one more squeeze, and then released him. "It's so good to have you home, Sawyer. All my boys. Here at last."

He glanced down at the slight tremor in his mother's voice. She had an indomitable spirit, but he could see the toll the last few months had taken on her too.

"It's good to be back, Ma."

She smiled, though it didn't mask the sadness in her eyes.

Then Vicky's gaze traveled to his left. "Hello, Leah, dear. We missed you at the last Ladies Auxiliary meeting at the fire hall."

"I'm sorry I couldn't make it. I had a parent-conference meeting that ran long."

Guilt suffused Sawyer as he glanced at her. Leah's face was red from trying to break up the fight, and it was clear she was uncertain of her place. Sam was right. He *was* an asshole.

His mom was kind enough not to notice. "No problem. I signed you up to help me in the kitchen at the yard party if that's okay."

"Sure, Mrs. Compton. I'd like that."

Vicky's smile grew, and she shook her head. "Good heavens, girl. How many times have I told you to call me Vicky?"

Leah shrugged good-naturedly, but didn't reply.

JD cleared his throat. "Welcome home, son."

Sawyer took a steadying breath, and then headed toward the porch. When he hit the top of the stairs, his father was there, relying on the support of a walker to remain upright. Sawyer tried to ignore the fucking thing, refusing to believe his father needed it.

JD reached over the walker and wrapped him in a surprisingly strong embrace. His hard hands slapped at Sawyer's back, and he grinned. No matter how much his father's physical appearance had changed, his old man could still give the toughest man-hugs in history.

"I'm here to stay."

His father's face darkened. "Not because of me—"

Sawyer shook his head. "No. I'm done with the Coast Guard."

"Thought you were going to be a rescue swimmer?"

Sawyer shrugged. That had been the plan. In fact, he'd spent eight weeks at sea training for a position he couldn't accept. "I'm coming home. I've missed this ranch."

JD looked like he might argue, but looked away from Sawyer to glance at Leah. "I see."

Damn old man. He never missed anything. Sawyer was grateful at least that hadn't changed, but he wondered how he would explain his relationship with Leah to his family. His father was obviously aware of part of what had solidified his decision to return to Wyoming, but Sawyer's mind had been made up before he'd reconnected with Leah in L.A.

"Thought you were hell bent on a life at sea?"

"I was." Sawyer hadn't told anyone—not even Leah—the real reason for his resignation from the Coast Guard. "There was an incident."

JD narrowed his eyes.

Vicky climbed the steps to stand beside them. "Sawyer? What happened?"

He swallowed heavily, wondering how he could explain. "We went on a rescue call a few weeks ago. A man fell overboard while he was on an excursion with his family. He hit his head on the way down. My ship was close. Call came through and we were there in minutes. I went into the water to fish him out."

Sawyer had arrived too late. When he'd gotten the man's body on board, his captain had been there to break the news of his death to the family. It wasn't Sawyer's first time witnessing such a sad occurrence, but the man had a young son—only eleven years old. Sawyer had seen the boy's face when he realized his father was dead. Whether it was an odd coincidence or an omen of things to come, Sawyer hadn't been able to erase that boy's response—the bleakness, the sheer agony—from his mind. The event had made him long for JD, for his brothers, for time.

The memory of the boy's eyes had jerked Sawyer out of a sound sleep too many nights, trembling with a cold sweat. Sawyer suspected he'd see those same eyes if he looked in the mirror right now.

"The man didn't make it. I realized I wasn't cut out for that life."

JD shook his head. "I don't agree with that assessment and something tells me I got the Reader's Digest condensed version of that story."

Sawyer smiled sadly. There was no way he could tell his father exactly what had prompted his return to the ranch. Not now. "Honest, JD. That's all there is to tell."

Vicky placed her hand on Sawyer's face. "You're a young

man, Sawyer. Only twenty-five. You have plenty of time to find a path that will make you happy in life. I'm glad you came home in the meantime."

He bent down and kissed his mother's cheek. He'd missed her more than he could say.

His kiss pleased her, as her smile widened, reaching her eyes this time. "Dinner's in the oven. Should be ready in about an hour. Why don't you grab your stuff and take it upstairs? Your room is ready for you. Leah, there's plenty of food. I hope you'll join us for supper."

Leah shook her head. "Oh no. I couldn't impose. I should get going." She walked to her car, popping the trunk with her key fob, then she grabbed Sawyer's duffel.

She wasn't getting away that easy. Sawyer followed her and took his bag from her. Out of earshot of his family, he leaned toward her. "Don't go." He owed her an apology. A big one.

She opened her mouth to argue, but he cut her off. His life was spiraling, plummeting away from him like a runaway train, and the only thing in the world that felt right was her. "Please, Leah."

"Leah Hollister," JD hollered from the porch. "Vicky's made two heaping pans of lasagna. If you don't stay and eat some of it, I'll be forced to choke down leftovers for the next three days."

Sawyer chuckled when his mother put her hands on her hips and feigned an evil glare.

"You love my lasagna, JD Compton, and you know it."

"You're right, I do—for a night or two, but merciful heaven, woman, you make enough to feed an army for a month."

Vicky spun toward the front door, opening the screen before shouting over her shoulder to Leah. "Now you have no choice but to stay. After all, someone has to eat JD's share since he'll be getting bread and water. If he's lucky."

She went into the house as JD blustered a fake complaint. Leah was right. The more things changed, the more they stayed the same. Sawyer chuckled.

His father rolled his walker toward the door, but he stopped at the threshold. He gave each of his sons a steely-eyed glare. "No more fighting. I may be sick and you may be grown men, but that doesn't mean I won't take each and every one of you out to the fencepost for a visit with my belt if you start throwing punches again. I won't have your mother upset. Understood?"

Though they all knew it was an empty threat, Sawyer watched his brothers nod solemnly. Whether it was today, or a year from now, they'd do their best to honor that promise to their father. It was no secret their mother would be devastated enough by the loss of her husband. Dissention in the family would kill her quicker than the cancer gnawing on his father's pancreas. A ranch, even one as sprawling as their holdings, would be a small place for four strong-willed Compass brothers. Somehow, they'd make it work.

When JD's gaze landed on Sawyer, he followed suit.

JD returned to the house, and Sawyer released a long, hard breath. "Fuck," he muttered so softly only Leah heard. His heart was beating too hard, and he was struggling to take a deep breath. He needed...

Leah placed her hand over his where it rested against the car. "It will be okay."

He lifted his face to hers and revealed too much when her eyes widened. He needed *her*. Now.

She shook her head. "Your whole family is here," she whispered.

"I don't care."

"Be practical," she pleaded.

"No."

"Sawyer?" Sam approached the car warily.

Sawyer looked at his brother and the ice-cold pain he'd experienced since seeing JD was replaced by anger so hot it singed.

"It's not a good time, Sam. You heard JD. He doesn't want us to upset Mom. Right now, I can't look at any of you without needing to beat the shit out of you, so step off."

Sam nodded stiffly. "Fine. But eventually you're going to have to cool down enough to let me enlighten you on a few things."

Sawyer shrugged. "Later. Not now."

Sam turned his attention to Leah. "Hey, Leah. Sorry you had to see all that."

She smiled at his twin, and Sawyer felt that familiar nagging jealousy. He knew it was impractical, but his emotions were on system overload.

"It's okay." Leah's face softened, her eyes filled with compassion. "It's a rough time for everyone."

Sawyer swung his duffel over one arm while grasping Leah's hand with his free one. He headed for the house when Silas stepped into his path.

"You're pissed off, Saw. I get it. But you're wrong to heap all the blame on Sam's head."

Sawyer gave his oldest brother a nasty smile. In the past, he'd looked up to Silas as much as he did JD. He'd emulated his older brother, tried to be like him. Right now, that admiration was gone, replaced with hurt and anger. "Oh, don't worry, Si. Sam's not the only one with a day of reckoning coming."

He stepped around his brother, enjoying the shocked expression on Si's typically set-in-stone features. He'd never dared to face off against his older, bigger, tougher brother before, but things had changed.

"God dammit, Saw. Don't you think it's time you took a minute and listened?"

Sawyer's vision blurred with fury and grief. Too much had happened too fast. He couldn't take one more thing. He honestly couldn't. "Not now, Si."

He wasn't sure what his brother saw in his face, but Silas nodded and stepped out of his way.

He continued to drag Leah into the house and upstairs to his room, not bothering to acknowledge the fact she was struggling pretty hard against him. When they entered his room, he tossed his duffel on the floor, then shut the door and locked it.

He tried to take a deep breath, but he was lost.

"Jesus, Saw."

He glanced up and saw Leah's pretty face, the concern written in her eyes. Common sense flew out the window.

"Lift that skirt."

She shook her head. "You're crazy if you think I'm going to have sex with you here while your whole family is downstairs. You've been home less than ten minutes and you've had a fight with all your brothers, seen your dad's illness up close and personal and pissed off every single woman on the ranch. Don't you think it's time you took a breather?"

Leah clearly didn't understand. She was his fresh air, his saving grace. He closed his eyes, wishing he could think of another way to escape the dark.

When he spoke, his voice was ragged. "I don't need a

breather. I'm going to tell you one more time to lift that skirt, Leah. You know what to say if you don't want that."

He wondered what he'd do if she gave him her safe word. For the first time in his life, he wasn't sure he could guarantee he'd respect the rule. He needed the sweet oblivion she could offer. Everything she'd said was true. As far as homecomings went, he'd managed to score the world's worst. But she was wrong about the cure. She was it. She would always be it.

She slowly lifted the hem of her short skirt. "We have to be quiet, Sawyer. I'd be mortified if your mother knew—"

He silenced her with a hard kiss. "We'll be as quiet as the sea on a calm morning. I promise." Tugging at the waistband of her panties, he shoved them down. He unzipped his jeans and pushed them to his knees. "Bend over the mattress. I'm afraid this is going to go too fast."

He'd taken her this morning against the wall of the bedroom in L.A. He hadn't planned it, but as they'd gathered up their things, intent on heading to the airport, his anxiety got the better of him. He'd taken her roughly, shoving the crotch of her panties out of the way and fucking her hard. Leah had given as good as she got, digging her nails into his shoulders, driving him wild with her demands. They'd come together quickly and the memory of it was the only thing that had gotten him through the too-long flight home.

He ran his hand along his erection. Within seconds, Leah was draped over his bed, her round ass beckoning him. He itched to lay his palm against her soft skin, but there was no way he could spank her without his family hearing the smacks or Leah's loud cries. She was a vocal lover, her screams and dirty demands never failing to turn him on even more.

He spread her ass with his hands and saw the proof of her desire smeared on her thighs. He aroused her, turned her on. It was a heady feeling—one he thought he'd never get used to. He placed his cock at the wet opening of her cunt and pressed forward in one long, hard motion. Leah groaned and Sawyer grinned.

If anyone was going to have a problem keeping quiet, it wasn't going to be him. He pulled his T-shirt over his head and dangled it in front of her face. "Maybe you'd better stuff this in your mouth, rose."

She shot him a dirty look over her shoulder, prompting him to retreat and return with a hard thrust. She cried out loudly.

"Fuck," she muttered as she took the shirt from him, biting down on the material. Christ, he was never washing that shirt again.

The sound of a radio drifted down the hall from Seth's room and Sawyer grinned, despite himself. Even after his asinine behavior outside, Seth had his back, helping to drown out what he and Leah were up to.

He began to pound inside her body, taking care not to shake the bed too hard. Gripping her hips, he enjoyed the image of her ass moving toward him. She'd mentioned a few times in the past being unhappy with her weight, but Sawyer couldn't see why. She had the perfect hourglass shape.

Leah thrashed beneath him, adding her own movements to the rhythm. Within minutes, Sawyer was on the verge of exploding. He reached around Leah's waist and pressed on her clit. He'd become obsessed with the tightness of her pussy milking him as he came. He needed that sensation as much as he needed food and air and water. She forced more of his shirt in her mouth as her groans grew louder.

The muffled sound of her cries drove him as crazy as her screams.

"Can't hold on, rose. Come for me. Come with me."

Her pussy clamped down the moment he issued the invite. His balls constricted, and his cock exploded as he filled her with his come. He'd never taken a woman without a condom before Leah, but he refused to put any barriers between them. Ever.

With his climax, the turmoil of the afternoon seemed to drift away. A few minutes in her arms and his sea legs returned.

He took a deep breath and let the calm descend, relishing it.

After a few moments, Leah's arms stopped supporting her and she fell forward onto the mattress. He followed her.

She pulled his T-shirt out of her mouth. "I can't believe I did that."

Sawyer chuckled. "Might be more correct to say *we* did that."

She attempted to dislodge him. He rolled to the side, watching as she left the bed. "I must be out of my mind. We're in your family's house. I'm not this kind of girl, Sawyer. How can I look JD in the face again? What if your mother heard? What if she tells *my* mom?"

Sawyer fought to restrain his mirth when he saw the genuine panic on Leah's face. "We're not still in high school, Leah. We're adults. There's nothing wrong with what we did."

She hastily set her clothing to rights. "Your family's going to think I'm a slut."

He frowned, rising quickly. "No. They're not. We're friends. There's no reason why they wouldn't think you just offered me a ride from the airport."

She raised her eyebrow and gestured to the mussed-up bed.

He chuckled. "Well, I guess they *would* have thought that.

Now they'll probably assume you're my girlfriend."

"But I'm not."

Sawyer shrugged. "Leah. I don't have all the answers right now. Does it really matter what other people think?"

"I don't like deceiving your family."

Sawyer panicked. If she insisted they call a halt to things now, he wasn't sure what he'd do. "I'm not finished with you, Leah. I wish I could offer you more, but right now, with my life such a mess, this is the most I have to give."

She plopped into a chair in the corner tiredly. "I'm not asking for more, Saw. I'm not ready for this to end yet either."

He breathed a sigh of relief as she looked around his bedroom, her gaze taking in every detail. He followed her visual tour, wondering what she was thinking as she looked at his old football trophies, the posters of cars and bikini-clad girls.

Now that he was moving home to stay, it was definitely time to update the décor. "Guess it's obvious I haven't been home much since I graduated."

She smiled. "It's a nice room. Big one. I sort of assumed you'd shared a room with Sam."

Sawyer shook his head. "We did when we were kids. It was fun then. We had bunk beds and all kinds of toys and shit. As we got older, we needed our own space. Good thing there are plenty of rooms in this house. Puberty hit Sam hard."

Leah laughed. "Just Sam?"

Sawyer shrugged, but didn't respond. "We probably would have killed each other if we'd had to share a room throughout high school."

"I never had my own bedroom."

He sat on the edge of the mattress. "Really? You're an only child."

114

"We couldn't afford more than a very small apartment. When I was little, I slept in my mom's room with her. As I got older, I claimed the living room so I could have my own space and I slept on the couch."

He stared at her. "Leah, how did I not know all of this about you when we were younger?"

She shrugged. "I was embarrassed, Saw. Didn't you ever wonder why I never invited you to my home to play?"

He raised his hands. "I'm a guy, Leah, and obviously not prone to thinking too much or being very observant."

She laughed. "Maybe, but I can't let you carry all that weight around. I was really good at shielding certain things about myself."

He wasn't sure why, but he was hurt by her deception. "Why wouldn't you tell me? I didn't care if you had money or a nice house."

"Things that mattered when I was a teenager seem silly to me now. I wish I knew why. I think I looked at you and saw so many things that I wanted—a big family, a nice house, a comfortable life. When I was with you, I was able to forget that I didn't have those things for a little while."

He could understand wanting to forget. It was a feeling he was becoming far too familiar with.

He gave her a seductive smile. "So, what's your sleeping situation now?"

She laughed. "Well, I'm not sleeping on a damn couch these days if that's what you're asking. Once I got a job at the elementary school, I moved into my own very spacious one-bedroom apartment and spent part of my first paycheck on a slightly used double bed someone was selling at a yard sale." Her smile grew. "I can still remember my first night in that big bed all by myself. I felt like the Queen of England."

He shook his head, grinning like a fool at her silly story. He'd taken so much for granted in his life, the roof over his head, the food on the table. Even his family... JD's health. He'd assumed all those things would always be there for him.

Leah had worked her ass off for every single thing she'd ever owned. *A rose in a field of dandelions.* JD must have known about Leah's struggles, known how truly remarkable she was.

Sawyer vowed then and there he'd find a way to make Leah's life easier for her.

Vicky's voice called up the stairs. "Dinnertime."

Sawyer grabbed a fresh T-shirt from his bag and put it on. He held out his hand. "You ready?"

She hesitated, and then took it. "You sure we should let them assume we're in a relationship?"

He smiled, pulling her closer. "I'm sure, girlfriend. Besides, why would that be such a bad thing?"

"What if they disapprove?"

Sawyer nodded. "That's a definite possibility."

Anxiety covered her face, but Sawyer didn't let her off the hook.

He kept his face straight as he continued, "Truth of the matter is JD will probably look you straight in the eye and tell you, you can do better."

Leah huffed loudly and punched him in the arm. "God, will you be serious?"

"I am. You can do a hell of a lot better than me, Leah. Shit. As of today, I'm an out-of-work guy living with his parents."

She laughed, then rubbed her chin thoughtfully. "Hmm. You raise a good point. Wow. Maybe I would be smart to move on. I need to consider this."

He tugged her closer. "Yeah, well, don't think too hard. I may not know much about my immediate future, but I can tell you this for certain. You're in it."

She smiled and he thought he saw a light sheen of tears in her eyes. "Sounds good."

They entered the dining room hand-in-hand. Hers trembled slightly as they discovered the rest of the family seated around the table. Even Sawyer had to admit the Comptons were an intimidating sight when they were all together. It didn't help that the family appeared to have doubled since the last time he was home.

He pulled her to the empty seat next to his. "Mom, Dad, look who I ran into in L.A."

Vicky grinned as Sawyer pulled out Leah's chair for her. "I was wondering where you two met up. Well, I guess I'll do the introductions considering some things have changed since the last time you were here, Sawyer."

Vicky started around the table. "Of course, you both know Lucy, Colby and Silas. Leah, I know you've met Jody, but Sawyer, I don't think you've had the chance to meet Seth's fiancée."

"Fiancée? Wow." Then Sawyer gave his future sister-in-law a wicked grin. "Well, let's say I've met parts of her, Ma. Her feet mainly." He was dying of curiosity to figure out how his brother had convinced the lovely brunette to marry him considering the last time he'd seen Jody, Seth had kidnapped her.

Sam snickered as well, obviously recalling the video chat where the brothers had spotted the lovely—and naked—Jody tied to Seth's bed. As much as Sawyer wanted to hold back, he couldn't resist laughing with his twin.

"Watch it, Saw," Seth warned.

Sawyer spotted the opportunity for revenge and filled Leah

117

in on the first time he'd seen Jody.

Seth shook his head, but Sawyer could tell his story wasn't new to anyone at the table as his other brothers were quick to jump in to add a detail or two. Even JD contributed a bit.

"Leah, I'm going to tell you I always credited you for being a bright girl. Seeing you here with my rascal of a brother has me reconsidering that," Seth said.

Leah laughed as Sawyer leaned closer to her, whispering, "And here I thought it would be JD warning you away."

JD, the wily old fox, heard him. "Me? Why the hell, ahem, pardon ladies. Why the heck would I tell her to stay away from you, Sawyer? I figure she's about the best thing that could happen to you."

Leah blushed. "Thank you, Mr. Compton."

JD put his fork down and leaned against the chair. "Blast it all, girl. Vicky and I have been telling you since you graduated from high school to call us by our first names. If you're gonna start dating our son, I'm going to have to start insisting harder. It's JD."

Leah looked uncomfortable. Sawyer decided he'd better lead them to safer waters. "We only ran into each other again a couple days ago, Pa. We're getting reacquainted."

"That's right," Leah added.

JD nodded. "Dating or not, I'd still like you to call me by my first name."

She looked at JD and gave his father a friendly smile. "Okay."

JD narrowed his eyes, his voice gruff, commanding. "Don't say okay, darlin'. Say *JD*. Let me hear it."

"Wow." Leah looked from JD to Sawyer and back again. "Uncanny resemblance. Never noticed it until now, JayDee," she added with a blush as she stressed his father's name.

Vicky laughed. "Didn't take you long to figure that out, Leah. Sawyer is the spit of his father, and I don't mean looks-wise."

Silas leaned forward. "Can we finish the introductions so I can eat? I'm starving."

Sam took Cindi's hand. "You both know Cindi, but what you don't know is we're getting married. I proposed to her last night, and she said yes."

Leah squealed with delight. Obviously she was better friends with the ranch bookkeeper than Sawyer realized. Sam wrapped his arm around Cindi's slim shoulders, and Sawyer was blown away by the true contentment on his brother's face.

"You're engaged too? Jesus. Two months ago, you were climbing the ladder to success in New York."

Sam looked at Cindi. "I finally realized there's more to happiness than money. Cindi taught me that."

Sawyer's mind whirled as he took in all the changes that had occurred since he'd been gone. The last time they'd all been here together had been the night Silas said he was leaving the ranch, heading north to Alaska. Fifteen at the time, Sawyer had been devastated. He'd felt like his family was being ripped apart at the seams. He'd been wrong.

Now rather than departing, they were all running back for a different reason and Sawyer understood what it meant to truly be torn apart. He glanced at his father and wondered how they'd survive without him.

He turned to his twin. "Congratulations, Sam."

Vicky launched into details of the double wedding they were planning for Seth and Sam and their lovely ladies while JD served the lasagna. For a little while, Sawyer was almost able to pretend that everything was normal.

"Do you still play the guitar, Leah?" Sam asked.

Leah smiled and nodded.

"As I recall, you were really good," Seth said.

She shrugged. "I'm okay, I guess. I'm afraid most of my strumming happens in the classroom these days. I play a mean *Insy Weensy Spider.*"

Cindi laughed. "I was hoping we could ask you to play something a little more contemporary at the wedding. You have a beautiful singing voice."

Leah sobered up. "You want me to perform at the wedding?"

"Of course," Cindi replied.

Sam looked concerned. "Is that going to be a problem?"

Leah shook her head. "No, not really. I'm flattered."

Cindi touched Sam's arm as she leaned toward Leah. "I talked to Jody this afternoon, and we think it would make the wedding really special."

"Okay. Then I'll do it. When's the big day?"

Every voice at the table except his and Leah's answered in unison. "Weekend after next."

Sawyer choked on his beer, rising quickly. "In two weeks? Were you even planning to fucking invite me to *that*?"

His anger resurfaced. It felt like everything in his family was changing, but no one had bothered to clue him in. Everyone was moving forward, heading toward something while he was treading water simply to keep his head above the surface. The feeling of drowning pressed down on him, and he needed air.

"Dammit, Sawyer. You don't understand." Sam stood as

well, but Sawyer had had enough surprises to last him a lifetime.

He lifted his hand. "No, I guess I don't." He looked at Leah. "I'm sorry, rose. I can't be here right now. I need a minute."

He could see in her face that she understood. "Alone?"

He nodded. Before anyone else could issue a protest, he left the dining room as the headache he'd held at bay all day unleashed itself on him.

The screen door slammed behind him before he could catch it. He actually paused for a moment, expecting his mom to yell at him. When the chastisement didn't come, he continued until he reached the edge of the yard.

He took the dirt path that meandered through the woods and led to a small creek, letting the moon light his way. He was overcome with guilt for leaving Leah alone with his family. While they'd be nothing but courteous to her, he knew she'd been uncomfortable going in. Yet another way he'd fucked up his grand return.

He sighed heavily. Tonight had proven one thing. He wasn't fit to be anyone's boyfriend—pretend or otherwise. He hadn't been kidding with Leah earlier. He had no job, no home, nothing to offer a woman except misery and anger. For Leah's sake, he needed to cut her free and end the relationship before he hurt her. Yet, even as the thought crossed his mind, he knew he wouldn't.

He picked his way gingerly through the dark woods. His family had looked so content at dinner. Despite all the bad stuff going on, they'd pulled together. Ordinarily, Sawyer would have been a part of it all, but tonight, he'd felt like an outcast.

He wondered when he'd become persona non grata in his family and how in the hell he could get back in.

Chapter Seven

The next few days passed in a blur as Sawyer threw himself into his chores. His mother was ruling the ranch with an iron fist, keeping his brothers and the hands hopping with wedding preparations. The big event was going to take place in the backyard and he'd spent every waking minute of every day since he'd returned home mending large tents, building an arch, cleaning up the yard and planting flowers.

He'd been cordial to his brothers, though none of them had said more than a few words in passing, usually in regards to whatever task they were working on. He knew he should break the ice, but he was struggling to find the words. Seeing JD so sick was gnawing away at his insides. He was fucking pissed off. Why did this have to happen to his dad? JD was one of the best men he'd ever known and he didn't deserve this fate, this suffering. It seemed like anger was the only emotion he could manage. He was surly and miserable and, unfortunately, his brothers were catching the brunt of it. He sure as hell couldn't let JD see how much he was hurting.

Every evening after dinner, he'd sit in the living room with JD and Vicky, watching TV, talking and catching up. After the initial shock of seeing his father's illness wore off, Sawyer was relieved to discover his father's spirit was still strong. Most nights the TV ended up on mute as he and JD reminisced about the "old days" or swapped funny stories about stuff that had happened since Sawyer joined the Coast Guard. Vicky always teased them for their ability to tell the biggest fish stories she'd ever heard. One night she declared they were neck in neck in the bullshit race, which prompted them to spin longer and more ridiculous stories. Sawyer had gone to bed that night with sore stomach muscles from laughing so hard.

Leah went back to work the day after they returned to Wyoming. He'd called her to offer an apology for storming out of the dining room. She'd graciously accepted it and they'd called each other a few times since then. Mainly, they talked about their days and she shared cute stories about her students. She clearly had the patience of a saint to work with such young kids day in and day out.

He ached to see her again. Regardless of his gut telling him the timing was wrong to embark on an affair, he was going to weaken. He needed to see her, talk to her, touch her. He was holding on to too much anger and agony. He was about to explode. Leah found a way to balance him, to bring him peace.

As he rolled up the driveway toward the barn in the farm pickup, he suspected his luck at avoiding a confrontation was about to run out. Cindi stood at the barn door, waiting for him. He climbed out of the truck, approached the flatbed and pulled down the tailgate. He'd driven into town to borrow some chairs from the fire hall for the wedding.

"Hey." Cindi walked up to him. "Need some help?"

He'd love it, but he didn't think he was going to like how much that assistance would cost him. "No thanks. I got it."

She shrugged. "Too bad. Need a break from the books."

He nodded, hoping to distract her. "Figure we can stack them in the corner of the barn until closer to the wedding day. They'll be in the way if we try to set them up too soon."

"Good idea." She took one of the four metal chairs he'd off-loaded and led him to a clear patch in an empty stall.

They started stacking them, working in silence for a few minutes as they carried chairs from the truck to the barn.

Cindi actually held her tongue long enough for him to think he might dodge the bullet. He should have known better.

"You know, you're going to have to talk to Sam eventually. How else is he going to ask you to be his best man?"

Sawyer paused in the midst of his chore. "Figured he had Silas lined up for that."

Cindi threw him an exasperated glance. "Silas is Seth's best man."

"So he can do double-duty. He'll already be standing there."

Cindi added her chair to their growing pile none too gently, the metal clanging loudly. "Damn it, Sawyer. You're messing up my wedding."

He pushed his cowboy hat back on his head and glared at her. "I am? Well, forgive me, darlin'. Here I was thinking I was working my ass off for your special day. Guess I didn't realize lugging chairs and flowers and mulch and fucking china all over kingdom come was ruining things for you."

Cindi had been a permanent fixture on his family's ranch for over two years. They had always enjoyed a comfortable friendship, playing rummy and hanging out whenever Sawyer was on leave. He was still trying to wrap his head around the fact Sam was marrying her. Not that he didn't think they were a good match. Truth be told, Cindi was perfect for his brother. If only it weren't all happening so fast.

"Don't play dumb with me. You know what I'm talking about. None of that matters when you're hurting the man I love. Sam is miserable. How long are you planning to keep up the silent treatment?"

Sawyer crossed his arms. "I figure he gave it to me for about eight weeks. That should work for me too."

Cindi sighed. "Our wedding is in nine days, and for some

reason I'm failing to understand more by the day, Sam is desperate for his twin brother to be his best man. Believe me, he's kicking his own ass way harder than you ever could, questioning every move he made the last couple of months. He tried to call you—several times—despite the fact JD forbade him to. JD insisted you would have your shot at that new position."

That sounded like JD. His father wouldn't let anything come between his son and a promotion—not even his own failing health. "Doesn't matter what JD said. Sam's my twin. He should have known I would want to be here."

"Clear the fury out of your ears and listen, Sawyer. No one could understand you more than Sam and me. My family didn't even tell me my mom had cancer until she'd already died and my father blew his brains out rather than live without her. You think I'd wish that on anyone? That I would have let you experience the hell I did? Never saying goodbye..."

Oh, fuck. Sawyer couldn't help himself. He cupped her elbow in his palm, steadying her until she shook the tears out of her eyes. "Christ, Cindi, I'm sorry. I didn't know."

"No shit. Did you ever stop to think about what Sam's been going through the last couple months?"

"Is everything all right in here?" Jake, one of the long-time ranch hands, poked his head into the stall where they stood. Sawyer didn't remember the surly guy looking quite so thunderous in the past.

"Just fine, thanks." Cindi painted on a brave face. "Could you please take the files on my desk up to Sam at the main house?"

Jake nodded and shuffled out.

"Cindi, listen—"

"No, Sawyer. Hear me out and maybe you'll pull your head out of your ass before it's too late. We're all living on borrowed

125

time these days. JD hates seeing you at odds. He's important to me too, you know?"

The bare torment in her gaze ripped through him like a fishing spear. JD had noticed? He thought he'd hidden his anger better since the scene at the dining-room table.

"God, I'm—"

She shushed him before he could beg forgiveness.

"Zip that big mouth and open your ears. There was a hell of a lot more falling apart in Sam's life than JD's illness. Did you know he lost his job in New York?"

Sawyer reared back. "What? How? There's no way that firm would fire Sam. He was the best thing to ever happen to them." He'd assumed his brother had quit to move home for Cindi and JD.

Cindi shrugged. Rather than answer, she planted her hands firmly on her hips. She reminded him of Vicky when she got riled up.

Sawyer tried to hide a grin. He wondered if his brother realized exactly what he was signing up for, marrying this spitfire.

His smirk seemed to incite her annoyance. She jammed her index finger into his chest hard enough to leave a bruise. "Maybe if you took a look around, you'd realize you are not the only person hurting here." Sawyer fought the instinct to retreat. "Sam needs you. He's been to hell and back these last couple of months, and I do *not* appreciate you making him feel any shittier than he already does. The only way we'll survive this is together. All of us."

"Fine."

His easy capitulation had Cindi narrowing her eyes. "Fine?"

He nodded. He couldn't argue against a single thing she'd

said. He *was* being a prick. He missed his brother. "Yeah. I'll talk to Sam."

"What about the head in your ass thing?"

He grinned. "I'll pull it out."

Cindi's scowl morphed into a big smile. She flung her arms around his waist and hugged him tight enough to make his eyes water. At least he swore it was that and not this yawning loneliness that had dogged him since Leah disappeared in a cloud of Wyoming dust Sunday night. He'd gotten back to the house too late to say goodbye to her.

"Great. I'll go find Sam and tell him you want to see him."

"I always wondered what it'd be like to have a sister." He gave her a squeeze. "Sam couldn't have picked me a better one."

"If you need a shoulder later, tomorrow, whenever, you know I'm here. I really do understand, *baby* brother."

Oh shit. He groaned. Not her too.

"Wait. Cindi—" Before he could stop her, she was out the door. "Jesus," he muttered, reeling as though he'd survived a tornado.

He'd decided to gather his thoughts as he unloaded more chairs when something in the corner caught his eye.

"Oh man. Hell yeah." He couldn't believe he'd forgotten one of the best things about being home. He jogged to the distant lump and pulled the cloth cover off his motorcycle. It was exactly as he'd left it. He must've been out of his mind to forget about *her*.

Sawyer stroked the sleek, sexy curves of his beloved Ducati. Leaving her behind had been the hardest thing about joining the Coast Guard. "How are you, my darling Jenn? God how I've missed you, girl."

"Talking to the motorcycle again? Jeez, bro. I sort of

thought you'd outgrown that stupid habit these past few years."

Sawyer rose. "Jenn and I have been away from each other for a long time. Have a little respect for the reunion. This is a pretty special moment."

Sam chuckled and hastily apologized for his thoughtless comment. It was always this way between them—the jokes flying. Sawyer realized he'd rather laugh with his twin than yell.

"How the hell did Cindi find you so fast?"

"I was in the house working a deal. Got a tip last night on a stock and I was checking it out."

Sawyer nodded. Same old brother. Sam, the financial whiz. "Going to make five million before you're thirty?"

Sam gave him a secret smile that made Sawyer think his brother had already achieved that goal. Sam remained in the doorway of the barn, shifting from foot to foot. Sawyer was overwhelmed with guilt for the wedge he'd driven between them.

He raised his hands in an act of surrender. "You don't have to worry. I'm not going to hit you again."

Sam snorted. "Yeah, well, I'm not taking any chances. A black eye is not on Cindi's list of approved accessories. You give me one before the wedding and she'll kill both of us." He leaned against the doorframe. "I prefer to keep my escape route close at hand."

Sawyer sat sidesaddle on his motorcycle, suddenly weary. Anger took too much energy. "I'm sorry I punched you."

Sam ran his hand through his hair. "I'm sorry I didn't tell you about JD. I picked up the phone a thousand times. Whenever I was ready to say it, I got your damn voice mail. Then when you did answer you sounded so happy, I just couldn't find the words to steal that away from you."

Sawyer understood. Even now, he couldn't bring himself to

say more than JD was sick. The idea of his dad dying was killing him. "What are we going to do without him?"

Sam shook his head. "Fuck if I know."

"I keep trying to wrap my head around it, but I can't make it stick. I look at him, and I can see how sick he is. Then he says or does something so completely JD, and I feel like everything's fine."

Sam nodded. "He's been good since you've been home. Lucy seems to think it's the wedding making him stronger. He's really looking forward to it."

Sawyer knew that to be true. It was one of the main things they discussed every night. JD was very pleased with Sam's and Seth's choices in brides. He talked about his future daughters-in-law like the sun rose and set on their shoulders. It comforted his father to know at least three of his sons had their futures settled. It was easy to look at Silas, Seth and Sam and know they'd found their paths.

While Sawyer was happy for his brothers, it was one more way he wasn't fitting in these days. He was twenty-five years old. He'd left the only job he'd ever known. He had no idea what he wanted to do now.

Add to that confusion, his relationship with Leah was too unsettled, too fucked up. His thoughts of her were a jumbled mess in his head. In the past, he'd had no problem separating sex and emotion. With Leah, those lines were blurred. Half the time he didn't think it was the physical comfort she offered that kept him coming back as much as the friendship. Lately she was the only person he could talk to. While he'd told her—and himself—it was just sex, just an exploration, he didn't think that was true.

He had no idea where she stood with their liaison. He'd been all over the place on the emotional scale since they'd crash-landed in each other's lives again. He'd been angry at his brothers, devastated about his father, and he'd exposed her to about every emotion in between. He didn't blame her for keeping her distance these past few days.

It was time for him to get a grip. He needed to start with Sam. "The wedding will be good for him. For all of us. Cindi's really something special. I'm happy for you, bro."

Sam grinned. "She's incredible. I'm not sure how I would have survived the last couple of months without her."

"She told me about your job."

Sam shrugged. "They fired me the same day I found out about JD."

"Jesus." Cindi was right. Sawyer had been an ass.

"Hindsight's twenty-twenty. Turns out losing my job was the best thing that ever happened to me. I belong on this ranch. With Cindi."

Sawyer snorted. "This from the guy who couldn't wait to get the hell out of Wyoming. Thought the bright lights of New York were going to hold you in their snare forever. Don't you miss your fancy high-rise apartment, the social life, the corner office? And what about that high-class bitch you were seeing...Belinda?"

"You never did like her, did you?"

"Hell, no." Sawyer grimaced. "Sorry but she seemed like a cold fish. Pretty packaging, but no substance inside."

"You can say that again. Nothing in that black heart except maybe ruthless greed. She's the one who got me fired. Slept with me, smacked me around then told our bosses I'd *coerced* her into divulging her strategies for the new growth fund."

"Fuck off. That bitch!"

Sam shook his head. "As for the rest, surprisingly, no. I

don't miss it. Not a bit. What about you? Are you happy about your decision to resign from the Coast Guard?"

Sawyer hadn't had time to think about what he'd left. He'd boarded the plane in L.A. and he hadn't looked back. "It's still too new. Not sure I've had time to consider the fact I'm not returning to work. Sort of feels like I'm on leave."

"I can understand that. Been a crazy week for you. Resigning from your job, coming home, finding out about JD. Seemed like there might have been some sparks between you and Leah, too. A lot to process in a few days. You think you'll be happy working on the ranch?"

Unfortunately, Sawyer did know the answer to that question. He wasn't a born rancher like Seth and Silas. While he loved the land, he didn't enjoy the prospect of working on it for the rest of his life. "Maybe."

Sam studied his face closely. Sawyer tried to paste on an impassive expression, but it was wasted on his brother. "That means no. I've been meaning to tell you there's a position open in town."

"Clerk at the mini-mart? Or maybe garbage man?" He wasn't joking. In a town as small as theirs, the options were limited. He'd do anything if it was an honest living, at least for a while. "What kind of position?"

Sam grinned. "Roberts is retiring as sheriff."

Sawyer chuckled. "In other words, Compton Pass needs a police force." Roberts was the only lawman the town required.

"Yep. JD and I were talking the other day. Seems to us you'd be a natural."

Sawyer rubbed the nape of his neck. A great deal of his Coast Guard work had involved boarding and searching boats suspected of running drugs. He definitely had some law-enforcement training. Hell, he probably had more experience

131

than the job called for. The only crimes he'd ever heard committed in Compton Pass involved cattle rustling, shoplifting at the local Piggly Wiggly and the occasional drunk in public. "That actually sounds pretty good to me. I'll look into it. Although God knows when I'll get a chance to see Roberts with all the shit we've got going on here to get ready for the wedding. Think Mom will give me an hour off for good behavior?"

"Probably, but you should plan on asking for that tomorrow. Tonight's agenda includes discussing the music with Leah. She's coming for dinner."

Sawyer tried to act nonchalant. "Oh. That's nice."

Sam laughed. "Jesus. Don't ever take up acting, man. That was a pathetic attempt at disinterest."

Sawyer scowled, standing up to scrutinize the gauges on his motorcycle. His brother read too much in his face and he was afraid of what he might see now. "Leah and I are renewing the friendship we had in high school."

"I don't remember you two having sex back then," Sam joked.

"So we're expanding on the relationship a bit."

Sam crossed his arms. "Yeah. It seemed obvious when you showed up here your *just friends* status had changed."

"I ran into her at a BDSM party in L.A."

Sam's eyes widened. "Damn. Wouldn't have expected her to go for that. She seems too sweet for the rough stuff."

Sawyer shook his head as he turned to face Sam. "There's a hell of a lot more to her than meets the eye. She's strong and honest and independent, but there's this vulnerability inside her that softens all of that and makes a man..." Sawyer swallowed heavily, wondering where the hell all that had come from.

Sam simply nodded. "I see."

Sawyer wished his brother would clue him in. "We're keeping it casual. It's a no-strings affair."

Sam grinned crookedly. "Is that right?" His twin's tone told him he didn't believe him.

His temper tweaked. "Damn straight."

Sam shrugged, not pushing the envelope. "Whatever you say."

"I'm serious, Sam. It's just sex. Jesus. How the hell could I even think about starting more with JD so sick?"

Sam stepped into the barn. "I don't think it's a question of timing, Saw. Or maybe it is. Cindi found me at the lowest point of my life and she built me up, brick by brick, until I was strong enough to stand on my own two feet again. She'd tell you I did the same thing for her. Looks to me like you could use a good carpenter these days. I'd suggest you not waste precious moments, like I did. It happened so fast it made my head spin. That didn't make it any less real."

"How fast is fast?" Could you fall in love after just one day? One amazing fuck?

"Uh, I don't like to brag but..." Sam wiggled his eyebrows. "I might have made love to her my first night home. Sure, I called it rebound sex, a way to numb the pain, or maybe just some crazy release from the disaster my life had morphed into overnight."

"But it wasn't any of those things?" Sawyer tilted his head.

"Nah. Well, maybe, yes. It was *all* of those things. And more." Sam stared at him so long he thought he might never speak again.

"So what are you trying to say?"

"I guess this... It's no use having big brothers if you don't

133

learn from their fuckups."

Sawyer didn't reply, wasn't sure how to answer. A few days ago, he'd been a man in charge of his destiny, his life. Now, the only word he could think to describe himself was shattered. How could he ask Leah for more when he didn't have a damn thing to offer in exchange? She'd come to that party looking for a man to take some of her burdens away, not to pile his own on her shoulders as well. No. She wanted to explore BDSM and that was all he could give her. He could take charge of her body, but that was all he had the strength to control. "I don't need anything except a warm, willing woman in my bed right now."

It was a lie, but Sam didn't argue with him.

Sawyer decided it was time for a diversion. "So, you ready for this wedding?"

Mercifully, his brother let the subject of Leah drop.

"Yeah. I can't wait to make Cindi mine. Permanently." Sam crossed the barn until he stood right in front of him. "That reminds me. I was sort of hoping you'd stand up with me. As my best man."

Sawyer offered his hand for a shake. "I'm glad you'll still have me. I can't think of anywhere else I'd rather be, bro. Thanks."

Sam nudged Sawyer's hand away, opting instead for a hug. Sawyer didn't realize until that moment how much he'd missed his brother.

"It's good to have you back, Saw."

Sawyer grinned. "Yeah. It's been a hell of a few days. Not sure it felt like home until right now."

Sam helped Sawyer finish unloading the chairs before sneaking off with Cindi shortly after lunch. Sawyer spent the rest of the afternoon moving from one mindless chore to the next.

With each passing minute, his body grew harder, hungrier as he anticipated Leah's arrival. When his watch told him school was out for the day, he camped out on the front porch. Sawyer glanced down the driveway when he heard tires on the gravel. He smiled. Finally.

He was waiting by her car when she opened her door and got out.

"Hiya, stranger." Her smile was genuine and friendly and the best thing he'd seen in days.

"Yeah, about that. What do you say we get reacquainted?"

"Now?"

He glanced at his motorcycle parked outside the barn and a plan took root. "I was thinking we could take a ride."

Leah looked tempted, but she hesitated. "I was supposed to talk to Jody and Cindi about the music for the wedding."

"Sam said you were staying for dinner. You can discuss it then. Just a quick ride, rose."

There were definitely two meanings to his suggestion, and the *quick* part wasn't going to be far from the truth. He was too hot, too ready for her. He'd never managed to hold off for long once he got into her sweet body. He waited for her response, holding his breath. What would he do if she said no? He recalled Seth's kidnapping tactic with Jody and realized the idea had merit.

If he were a gentleman, he'd step aside and let her head into his family's house untouched.

Pity was that wasn't going to happen. His inner alpha roared. For once, he took his brother's advice.

"I'm going to get a blanket and some rope from the barn. You stayed away too long, rose. It's time I remind you who owns this body."

She didn't reply, though her body gave him the only answer he needed. Her breathing turned shallow, and her nipples pebbled.

"Don't move."

Leah stood spellbound while Sawyer tied a large blanket to the rear of his motorcycle. Once it was secure, he straddled the bike and beckoned to her. "Hop on."

She took her place behind him, unable to resist a small scream when Sawyer turned the motor over and took off. The ride gave her too much time to think. Neither of them bothered to attempt a conversation that required yelling to be heard above the roar of the engine.

Sawyer had been waiting in the yard when she'd pulled up. Her heart soared when she'd seen him on the porch. The expression he wore today was a far cry from the last time they'd been together. She hoped his smile meant he'd patched up his differences with his brothers and was settling into being home again.

She clung tighter to him and enjoyed the feeling of his hard, sexy body as he drove the sleek motorcycle. He was wearing faded Levi's and a T-shirt. He'd exchanged his cowboy hat for a helmet. He took her breath away. Her urban cowboy.

For the past three days, she'd been climbing the walls—reliving, analyzing, fretting over every word they'd ever said to each other.

When they reached their destination, Leah pulled off her helmet and looked around. Sawyer had picked the perfect spot. They were flanked by a mountain on one side and miles and miles of pasture land on the other three. It felt like they were the only two people on the planet.

Sawyer unhooked the blanket and tossed it to her. "Pick us a good spot."

She roamed a few feet away, flipping out the soft material and spreading it on the grass.

Leah slipped off her shoes before sitting down.

Sawyer joined her. "Three days is too long."

She laughed when he uttered exactly what she'd been thinking. "I thought you'd be catching up with your family." She sobered as she remembered the scene in the dining room. "Everything okay?"

He nodded. "Yep. Patched things up with Sam this afternoon. Still need to track down Seth and Silas and set everything right there, but it's better."

"I'm glad."

"Sam asked me to be his best man."

She imagined Sawyer in a tuxedo and was grateful she'd agreed to sing at the wedding. There was no way she'd miss that sight. "Awesome."

She squeezed her legs together. Five minutes in his presence had her panties wet and her nipples hard. She needed to get a grip, but she couldn't help wishing he'd hurry things along.

Leah glanced at his motorcycle. "I can't believe you still own that silly bike."

Sawyer reacted as if she'd struck him. "Jenn is a Ducati, rose. There's absolutely nothing silly about a Ducati."

She placed her hand over her heart and feigned a swoon. "Oh my, how could I forget? It's a *Ducati*." She stressed the name, giggling. "That's the one you got for your birthday, right?"

He nodded. "Eighteenth. Worked my ass off around the ranch to earn money for half. JD said he'd pitch in the other half as the birthday gift."

"You came into town on it. I remember my mother joking around that you Compass brothers were reckless enough on horses and JD must be out of his mind to put you on that thing."

Sawyer laughed. "Is that why you couldn't go for a ride with me?"

Leah sighed. Sawyer had invited her out on his motorcycle that day and she'd never wanted to go anywhere so badly in her life. "No, that was actually my boss' fault. We were short-staffed at the diner."

Sawyer ran his finger along her arm. "Well, at least we got to make up for it today."

"Yeah." She hesitated for a moment, and then she said what was on her mind. "I always wondered what would have happened if I'd said to hell with it and gone with you."

"What do you think?"

The hungry look on his face proved he suspected the same thing she did. It wasn't long after that missed ride that she'd given into Les' invitation to relieve her of her pesky virginity. Would history have been rewritten if only she'd said yes?

"I think we both know." Leah shrugged and dismissed the thought. No use crying over spilt milk. "I can see the appeal of a motorcycle. That ride was a lot of fun."

"Riding is *very* fun."

She bit her lower lip. His eyes drifted from her face to her neck. She wondered if he could see her pulse, could tell how hard her heart was hammering.

It was difficult for her to think whenever he was near. Unfortunately, when she was alone, her brain kicked into overdrive and it had been giving her a run for her money the past three days.

He said he needed her. Actually, he needed the distraction she could provide. She was glad to be able to help him through this hard time. For once, her head was telling her to go ahead and submit to the sexy cowboy. She finally had a sex life—and it was a good one. Sawyer allowed her to explore the boundaries of her desires and he was opening her eyes to a whole new world of sensual bliss.

This time the problem was her heart. It was digging in its heels, demanding everything—Sawyer's body, his laughter, his compassion, his love.

He'd offered some, but not all. How long could she accept half without begging him for the rest?

Sawyer moved closer. He looked like a predator stalking its prey. "I'm not stopping, Leah."

"You're not?"

He shook his head.

"What if I say my safe word?"

His eyes narrowed. "Don't."

She struggled to take a breath. He constantly offered her the choice. This time, he wasn't.

She leaned forward, initiating the kiss before Sawyer could get to her. She gripped his hair tightly in her hands, attacking him with her lips, her teeth, her tongue. She was starving.

"Easy, rose. We can skip dinner and take all night if you need it."

He pushed her down on the blanket, taking the lead on the kiss and just like that, calm descended. The stress of work, her anxieties and insecurities all melted away and she put herself in Sawyer's oh-too-capable hands.

He came over her body, supporting the majority of his

139

weight on his elbows, while managing to cover every part of her. His legs shoved her knees apart as he claimed his spot in between them. Pressing down, he rubbed his denim-covered cock against her, letting her sense exactly what he was offering.

"God, Sawyer," she whispered.

His lips drifted along her cheek, nipping and licking the bare flesh at her neck. "I feel the same way. I need you so bad, Leah."

She dragged his T-shirt off. The second it hit the ground, she was back, touching him, memorizing every curve of his tattoos, every well-defined muscle.

Sawyer gripped her waist and spun until he was beneath her on the blanket. He used the position to give him the ability to undress her. He reached for the buttons on her blouse, but she beat him to the punch, pulling the silky shirt off. His hands engulfed her lace-covered breasts.

"Take off your bra."

She complied, pulling it slowly from her body, savoring his almost-feral gaze as she revealed her breasts little by little.

"Fuck," he muttered when she peeled the last bit away. "Come here. Feed them to me."

She straddled his hips, pressing down to find some relief for her aching pussy as she bent at the waist to give Sawyer the taste he'd requested.

He roughly grasped her breasts, moving from one to the other as he planted soft kisses and hard sucks on her tight nipples. She began to gyrate, thrusting against him, frustrated by the layers of clothing between them.

Sawyer continued to suck on her breasts, but one hand drifted down her side to lift her skirt. He raised it to her waist, and then gripped her ass, pulling her more firmly against him.

He chuckled softly. "I haven't indulged in dry-humping since I was a teenager. Forgot how good it feels."

She agreed as Sawyer tumbled them until she was beneath him. She was surprised when he made no move to take off his jeans or her panties. Instead he continued to rub their bodies together.

"Wonder who'll last longer."

She groaned. "Oh my God. Seriously? Sawyer, I'm about to explode. I need you to fuck me. I can't stand any more of this."

He leaned forward and bit her earlobe. "You're going to take exactly what I give you. Should we put a wager on it? We keep our pants on. First one to make the other come gets..."

He paused, letting her fill in the blanks. She finished the sentence without considering her answer. "Gets to be on top."

Sawyer grinned. "You a cowgirl at heart, rose? Giddyup?"

She hadn't really considered it one way or the other until she'd been above him. She'd spent far too much time on top in the past, the position never really bringing her much satisfaction. Something told her it would be different with Sawyer.

"Hell yeah."

He pinched her nipple, the touch making her groan. He was going to fight dirty.

"No other rules?" she asked.

He shook his head. "Do your worst, Leah. I'm ready for you."

Her laugh was short-lived when he pressed his cock against her pussy. He had the definite advantage. His denim was far thicker than her thin, silk panties and he knew it. He rubbed harder, his cock stroking nearly the entire length of her slit, paying special attention to her clit.

"This isn't fair," she said when his lips returned to her breasts.

He looked up at her and grinned. "Every night I close my eyes to go to sleep, I see your beautiful face, the way it looks when you come." He moved against her again, the rough denim creating enough friction to drive her out of her mind.

"I stroke my cock and remember you, your soft cries, your sweet scent. You drive me wild, Leah."

She threw her head back against the blanket. Her eyes drifted shut as she imagined him jacking off in his bed. It was a hot image.

"God, Saw."

"Come for me, Leah. Let me see it again. For real this time."

She wasn't sure what magic he'd worked on her, but his cock rubbing her slit and his command were the only triggers she needed. She conceded the prize and came—loudly. "Ohmigod. Ohmigod." She trembled, amazed by how quickly he'd brought her to this point. She gasped and struggled to catch her breath.

Sawyer's chuckle brought her back to reality.

"Hate to break it to you, cowboy, but I think that time, losing was way better than winning."

"Good point."

"Of course, we could always go for a draw." Placing her palm between Sawyer's cock and her body, she firmly applied as much pressure as she could muster to make sure he got plenty of sensation through the denim.

Sawyer cursed. Bingo. He liked her hand job. She recalled their conversation about the motorcycle, and she decided to up the ante.

"Imagine if we'd taken this ride the day you got your bike,

Saw. I would have liked to be your first. We would have ridden out here, sneaking onto the property so our parents wouldn't know."

Sawyer pushed his cock harder against her palm. He was enjoying her story.

"Of course, I would have been nervous since it was my first time too. You would know that and you'd take things slow. Kissing me for hours."

Sawyer bent down, offering her a kiss so sweet and innocent she almost believed her own words.

When he pulled away, she followed him, searching for more. Sawyer shook his head. "Tell me about that day."

She leaned back, tightening her grip on his cock. "You'd touch my breasts...above my shirt at first. But soon, you'd get bolder and slip your fingers beneath my T-shirt."

He mimicked her words, caressing her breasts almost shyly, a far cry from the no-holds-barred lover she was used to. "Do you like me touching you here?"

"Yes," she whispered.

"Would you let me see them? Kiss them?"

She nodded. Her heart raced when Sawyer picked up the game, reminding her so much of the boy he used to be. She was transported back in time, reveling in the opportunity to do things differently. To do them right.

"You're so pretty."

She closed her eyes, his compliment moving her.

He bent his head and softly kissed her breasts, worshipping them with delicate strokes. "Have you ever let another boy touch you here, Leah?"

She shook her head. "No one. Only you."

He gave her a boyish smile, then kissed her. He shoved her

hand more firmly against his cock. "I love your hand on me."

She let him guide her clumsy, innocent motions. "It's so big," she whispered.

He laughed. "Not really. You want to see it?"

"I'm afraid."

He took her face in his hands. "You don't have to be, Leah. I won't do anything you don't want me to."

She licked her lips and nodded. "I'd like to."

He rose until he was kneeling above her. Unzipping his jeans, he slowly pulled out his cock.

She bit her lower lip as she stared at him, the nervousness too genuine. What would she give to go back in time and have this day be real? "You should have been my first."

Sawyer grasped her hand and lifted her until she was sitting in front of him. She'd never seen him look so serious. "I'm going to make love to you, Leah. I *am* going to be your first."

Tears sprung to her eyes. He was right. She'd never made love before. In the past, she chosen badly, slept with men for the sex, not the affection. "I'm scared," she whispered.

He gave her a crooked grin. "So am I."

He pressed on her shoulder until she lay on the blanket. He bid her to lift her hips as he rid her of her skirt and panties. She'd been naked in front of him before, but she'd never felt this exposed.

He stood briefly to shed his own jeans and within seconds, he was on top of her. "We'll go slowly."

She accepted his soft kiss, sealing his promise.

She opened her legs and he placed the head of his cock the slightest bit inside. "I promise I won't hurt you."

She ran her thumb along his lower lip and prayed that was true. Right now, Sawyer held her heart in his hands and it would be far too easy for him to break it.

"I want to feel you inside me," she pleaded.

Sawyer moved slowly, each penetrating inch touching more than her body. He was piercing her soul, claiming far more than he realized.

Buried to the hilt, he stopped and kissed her. "Amazing."

She'd never considered herself anything special before, but in a few short days, Sawyer had her believing she truly was. They rocked gently, their bodies swaying in perfect harmony. Though they'd only been together a few times, they were already in tune with each other. Sawyer liked it when she stroked his back, and he knew it drove her wild when he kissed her neck. Over and over, he thrust into her body and she wondered if there'd ever been a more wonderful moment.

When she arrived at the point of no return, Sawyer was right there with her.

He pressed on her clit, his lips resting by her ear. "Come for me, rose."

Her body jolted beneath his, her muscles compressing his cock as he filled her. Neither of them moved, the power of the coupling too strong.

After several minutes, Sawyer stirred, pulling out of her body with obvious reluctance. "Jesus, Leah. That was..."

For once, she'd managed to leave him speechless. She liked that.

"Yeah, it was." She stared at his handsome face and the words she longed to say hovered at the edge of her lips. She opened her mouth, about to tell him how she felt when he grabbed his T-shirt and put it back on.

"You always find a way to make me forget my troubles. When I'm with you, it's like the whole world disappears. It feels so good. I don't know how I'd make it through these days without you."

She nodded, a lump growing in her throat. Distraction. How could she forget? She was his diversion. They played sex games together. That was all. She swallowed down her confession and tucked the pain away.

He needed her body. That was all. And for now, she wasn't strong enough to deny him that.

Chapter Eight

After their motorcycle ride, Leah and Sawyer had returned to the ranch for dinner with his family and Jody and Cindi had whisked Leah away to talk about music. That night had been an omen of things to come for the next week of Sawyer's life. The out-of-town guests started arriving a few days later and the wedding preparations shifted into high gear. The ranch house had been a hub of activity and as a result, he hadn't had two seconds alone with Leah. She'd come to visit several times, but whenever she showed up, Vicky, Jody and Cindi dragged her away with talk of the wedding. It was killing him.

Tonight, he was determined to grab a little private time with her. They'd done a brief wedding rehearsal, simply walking through the bridal party lineup. Jody and Cindi had decided they wanted the real day to feel natural, so apart from telling them who stood where, they hadn't covered much more. Sawyer was disappointed because he'd been looking forward to hearing Leah sing.

The rehearsal was followed by a special dinner. He had to admit his family knew how to throw a wedding. Sawyer had reconnected with quite a few old friends from town and had a long conversation with Roberts about what the sheriff position involved. The old lawman had seemed pleased when Sawyer expressed interest and invited Sawyer to shadow him one day next week. For the first time since returning home, Sawyer felt optimistic and excited about what his life here could entail. The sheriff job was something he could see himself doing happily for a very long time.

JD retired right after dinner. Sawyer worried about his father's wan face and his weakened breathing, but it was hard to stay down around JD. While his outward appearance had changed, his powerful personality still shone through. His father had warned them all to behave themselves, or if that wasn't possible, to have fun with the knowledge Vicky would have their asses out of bed—come hell or high water—at the crack of dawn. JD said they could do tomorrow hungover or not—the decision was theirs. Lucy and Seth had helped JD into the house. When Seth came back, he told them their dad insisted on being left in the recliner on the back porch for a little while. JD wanted to watch the dancing and listen to the music and the laughter.

Sawyer spent nearly an hour talking with Jody's father, Thomas, and her best friend, Paul, as well as Paul's partner, Chase. He'd heard a lot about all three men from his brother and he could see why Seth spoke so highly of them. Chase had them all busting a gut as he recalled the details of Jody's bachelorette party at a southern honky-tonk. Apparently it involved tequila, dancing on a pool table and ended with a brawl. God bless Texas!

However, Sawyer enjoyed watching Leah most of all. There didn't seem to be anyone in town who didn't know and like her. She chatted with the mother of one of her kindergarteners, caught up with some regulars from her days working in the diner, and spent lots of time laughing with Jody, Cindi and Lucy. His soon-to-be sisters had added Leah to their fold. Sawyer was grateful to them for that. Once the big event was over, he anticipated their matchmaking schemes would kick in. He'd only received this reprieve because they'd been so busy with everything else going on.

Sometimes he got the sense that Leah worried about his family's acceptance of her. He could only assume she still had lingering insecurities about her dirt-poor upbringing. Someday soon he was going to have to tell her his family didn't judge a person by what they had in the bank but rather by what they had in their heart. His family saw Leah as clearly as he did. She was generous, compassionate and kind and he ached to convince her of that.

Colby had dragged out some big speakers earlier in the day for tomorrow's reception. Stepping behind the table, he fired up the music, playing impromptu deejay for the evening. Sawyer laughed when Jake and a bunch of other ranch hands pulled Cindi into the middle of a fast-paced Texas two-step. Sam kept trying to cut in, but every time he approached, another ranch hand stole her away. Sawyer's head spun as he watched the dancing antics. He and Sam had spent a few afternoons catching up on the front porch. He'd known about Sam's penchant for group sex forever. Sawyer wasn't surprised when Sam mentioned that he and the hands weren't exactly shy about sharing Cindi. Apparently the time Sam spent in the big city hadn't changed his brother that much. Sawyer was comforted by that thought.

Sawyer caught sight of Leah sitting off to one side of the makeshift dance floor, laughing at the ranch hands. Sawyer thought about the deep sexual connection he'd made with Leah. He and Sam had gone off at eighteen to explore not only the world, but their darker sexual tastes. Now he was home again, and he realized what he'd been looking for had been here all along.

Leah looked lovely, achingly so. He hadn't managed to steal more than a few words with her all night, but that was about to change. A slow country ballad came on and he stood, intent on staking his claim. Before he could reach her though, Jake managed to beat him to the punch. The sexy cowboy spun her onto the floor and pulled her too close for Sawyer's comfort. He watched them for a few moments, his jaw clenching as a haze of red-hot anger permeated his body.

He took two steps forward, intent on beating Jake's smugness into the ground. The ranch hand whispered something in Leah's ear, and she blushed. Sawyer balled his fists. Game over.

"Hey, cowboy." It took Sawyer a moment to realize his path had been blocked. Looking down, he saw Beth, her head tilted to one side like she was posing for some fashion magazine. The girl had always had an over-inflated opinion of her looks, flipping her long blonde hair often, wielding it the same way a soldier did a weapon. Worst part was he'd fallen for it all—lock, stock and barrel—in high school. Damn, he'd been a dumbass.

She took a deep breath and made certain the action drew his attention to her barely covered breasts. Her tank top was cut so low she was leaving nothing to the imagination. He recalled the pretty yellow blouse Leah was wearing tonight. She'd left the top two buttons undone, treating him to peek-a-boo glimpses of her sexy cleavage. He preferred Leah's teasing to Beth's in-your-face obviousness.

"Hi, Beth." He'd managed to avoid her all night. Seth had apologized for inviting her when he realized how uncomfortable her attendance made Sawyer. Beth had taken her interest in horticulture class and turned it into a career. She was the only florist in town. Seth said Vicky had thought it only right to invite her since she'd done all the flowers for the ceremony.

"It's about time you got back to Compton Pass."

He wasn't sure if she was chastising him for leaving JD alone or issuing a flirtatious rebuke for leaving *her* alone. Both annoyed him. "Coast Guard duty called these last few years. I've been out at sea a lot lately."

She ran her hand suggestively along his chest. "Is that

right? Must've been lonely out there."

She took a step closer, whispering, "You know, now that you're home, maybe we should pick up where we left off when we were younger. I loved the things we used to do together."

Sawyer recalled the summer before he left for the Coast Guard. He'd begun to suspect some of the darker aspects of his sexuality, and he'd found a willing playmate in Beth. She loved having her ass spanked.

He sighed, equal parts regret and disgust as he recalled his non-discerning taste in women back then. For years, he'd drifted from bed to bed with faceless, nameless women searching for something he'd never found. While he liked the edge, the excitement of the act, at the end of the evening, he'd always been left wanting more.

He glanced at Leah, who was laughing at something Jake said. He hadn't felt that way with her. Ever.

He'd taken her out on his motorcycle, intent on tying her up and expanding her sexual boundaries. Instead, she'd thrown him for a loop with her virgin fantasy and he'd ended up making love to her. He hadn't lied about it being a first. She *was* his first in that regard.

He looked at Beth and knew his days of sleeping with strangers, with women who didn't mean anything to him, were over.

"I'm sorry. I don't think that would be such a great idea."

Her wolfish grin grew. "You know, I've grown up too, Saw. I've heard the rumors about you. I can take the harder stuff. Tie me up, whip me, force me. I promise you won't be disappointed."

He shook his head, wishing there was some easy way to let her down. "It's not that. It's not a good time. Not with the wedding, JD's illness..." *Leah.* He'd left the last unsaid, though

151

she was the only valid reason for his refusal.

"I could help you erase all of that from your mind."

He nodded. She probably could. But he realized he didn't want to forget it. If he was going to take control of his life, he needed to start by opening his eyes and accepting what was going on around him. "I'm not interested in forgetting. Excuse me."

The song had ended by the time he reached Leah's side. He forced himself to take a deep, calming breath when she hugged Jake and thanked him for the dance. The ranch hand tipped his hat, and then caught sight of Sawyer.

"Hey, Saw. Come to steal my girl away?"

Sawyer shook his head. "Nope. I'm here to reclaim *my* girl from you."

Jake wrapped his arm around Leah's shoulders, pulling her too close. Sawyer sensed Jake was purposely poking the bear, but he couldn't understand why. "Is that so?"

Sawyer narrowed his eyes in warning. "Yep. Sure is."

Jake shook his head. "You Compass brothers are something else. Think you can sashay back into town whenever you feel like it and grab up any pretty girl who catches your eye."

"Jake. You don't want to push me on this."

Jake shrugged, unconcerned. "Maybe I do. You see, I asked Leah for another dance and she agreed."

Sawyer turned to her, the jealousy he'd managed to lock away, resurfacing. It wasn't a comfortable emotion for him, but he couldn't shake loose of its grip.

"Sawyer—" Leah raised her hand, clearly afraid of what he might do.

"Take a walk with me, rose."

Jake stepped forward like he would interfere, but Leah moved faster. "Okay. Fine."

Jake looked at her. "You sure you're okay, Leah?"

She nodded. "Yeah. Sawyer and I have a couple of things we need to hash out. I'll only be gone a minute."

Jake gave Sawyer a hard look. "I'll be here."

Sawyer grinned and shook his head. "You'll be waiting a long damn time."

Leah took Sawyer's hand and dragged him away before Jake could reply. He let her draw him all the way to the front yard before he halted their escape.

"What the hell was that about?" she asked. "Jeez, Sawyer. Could you be a bigger caveman?"

The temper that had been simmering beneath the surface sparked and caught fire. "As a matter of fact, I can."

He grasped her hand and tugged her forcefully toward the barn, not stopping until they were at the base of the hayloft ladder. "Climb."

She shook her head. "No."

"Fine." He bent over, placed his shoulder to her middle and lifted her fireman style.

"What the hell—" Her protest was cut off when Sawyer climbed the ladder. He wasn't sure if it was shock or fear that held her still, but at this point, he wasn't going to ponder the question too deeply.

Once they reached the loft, he set her down. The second Leah's feet found solid ground again, her anger returned full-force.

"Have you lost your mind?"

"Yeah," he said. "I think I have. Doesn't matter though. You and I have an arrangement."

153

She put her hands on her hips. "Oh yeah? And what is that?"

He stepped closer. "I told you you're mine."

She scoffed. "Oh, stop with the Tarzan chest beating. We're fucking, Sawyer. Distracting each other from real life. That's all this—"

His head exploded. "Fucking?" The other night had been as far from fucking as it got. "Jesus."

His breath was labored, his heart beating rapidly.

Leah rubbed her temples wearily. "I need to go before we say something we—"

He blocked her path. "No. We aren't finished. Not yet."

She shook her head. "Sawyer, I can't—"

He cut her off. Covered her mouth with his and silenced her. Leah fought him for a split second before her hands stopped shoving against his chest and started caressing it. As he kissed her, he moved her back until they hit the edge of the pile of hay.

He looked at her. Her lips were swollen from his hard kisses, her face flushed. He'd never experienced this driving need to possess a woman so completely before. Obviously she didn't know the difference between fucking and making love. He'd show her.

"Kneel."

Leah obeyed without question. Sawyer's dominant side took over. He unzipped his jeans, shedding them and his shoes. He gripped his erection, holding it in front of her face. Leah licked her lips, her gaze glued to his face.

"Open your mouth."

Again, she followed his command. Sawyer moved forward, pressing the head of his cock inside. "You think this is fucking?"

She gave him a questioning look, unable to respond. Sawyer moved deeper, thrusting until he brushed the back of her throat.

Leah's hands gripped his ass, drawing him nearer with tight fingers. She swallowed his head and for a moment, Sawyer saw stars. He increased the pace. In the past he'd taken care, held back. He shouldn't have spared the effort. It was clear she didn't need his gentleness.

The thought sent a surge of anger through him, and he dragged his cock away. He reached under her arms to lift her. He wasn't being careful with her. He couldn't find that ability any more.

She'd killed him with her accusation. Hurt him more than he thought possible.

Once she was standing, he lifted her skirt, breaking the elastic on her panties and tossing them away. "Just fucking, right, Leah?"

She hesitated, looked confused. She nodded slowly. "That's all."

"So be it."

He pushed her to the wall of the loft, forcing her face-first against the wood. "Spread your legs."

She complied. Sawyer ran his finger along her slit. She was soaking wet.

He shoved two fingers into her tight cunt, and Leah groaned. He pounded them into her body. When her muscles began to flutter, signaling her orgasm, he removed them.

Leah cried out, but he silenced her with a slap on the ass. "You know the rules of our *fucking*."

He stressed the last word, and Leah winced. He was being

an ass, but he couldn't hold back his pain. This meant more to him. So much more. She hadn't felt the same way.

He took a step away, applying pressure on her shoulder at the same time he pulled her hips toward him. "Bend over."

Leah kept her hands flat against the wall, trembling slightly when Sawyer separated her cheeks. "I wish I had some lube. I'd fuck your ass right now."

"God," she whispered. "Please."

He spanked her again. "No."

He placed the head of his cock into her body, and she gasped. "Please, Sawyer."

"I know what you want, Leah."

He shoved inside with one hard blow. Only Leah's hands on the wall kept her in place.

Was she interested in Jake? Was she planning to end her affair with Sawyer to start a relationship with the ranch hand?

She was Sawyer's. He wouldn't let her go, wouldn't allow Jake to lay a fucking finger on her.

Mine. The word replayed in his head, the single syllable matching the rhythm of his rough possession. *Mine. Mine. Mine.*

Leah came loudly, her cunt squeezing his cock so hard he felt dizzy. It didn't stop him, didn't slow his pace. He needed her to know, to understand what it meant to belong to him.

Her second orgasm came quicker, accompanied by Leah's sobbing gasps for breath, for respite.

He lifted her slightly, taking care to remain in her body. With two awkward steps, he managed to get her to the pile of hay where he dragged her down to her knees. Throughout it all, he kept them connected.

Clutching her hips, he began anew, pummeling her body with thrust after deep, hard thrust. Leah's arms crumpled beneath her, her face rested against her hands on the floor. The new position opened her up even more, and he drove in faster.

When she came again, Sawyer was helpless to resist the impulse to join her. Her pussy squeezed his cock so deliciously tight, he feared she would bruise it.

They collapsed in a heap. Sawyer held his softening cock inside her, even as the truth of what he'd done crashed in on him.

He'd lost control. Taken her too roughly. He'd let his emotions drive his actions rather than his brain.

He wrapped his arms around her, spooning her in the hay. "Leah—"

She stirred, forcing his hands away. She disentangled from his hold so that she could turn to face him. "I'm sorry," she whispered.

He blinked, confused. She was apologizing to him? "Why? I was the one—"

She pressed her fingers to his lips. "I've been lying to you, Saw."

His heart stopped. "About what?"

She stood up, her face sadder than he'd ever seen it. He resisted the urge to drag her back into his arms.

It was clear she needed the distance. He moved slowly, his bare ass itchy as he sat on the hay. Leah pulled her skirt down and reclaimed her blouse.

Sawyer swallowed heavily. Had he physically hurt her?

Once she was dressed, Leah looked away.

"What did you lie about, Leah?"

"I let you think the sex was enough. I pretended I was fine with being your distraction."

He'd done the same. "Leah—"

"No. Please, let me say this. I've had a crush on you since we were kids. When we were at the party in L.A., all those childish feelings morphed into something deeper, something more. I know your family is going through a rough time and I'm wrong to lay all this at your feet now, but I can't continue this relationship anymore. I thought I could handle this better if we called it fucking, just sex. It didn't work. I can't be with you and pretend I don't care."

Sawyer was too shocked to move. Her heart was engaged too. She cared about him.

Leah rubbed her hands along her skirt nervously. "I saw you talking to Beth. I didn't like it."

"It was just a conversation."

She smiled sadly. "I know that, but it still annoyed me. It brought back those stupid emotions I had to deal with in high school. Insecurity, humiliation, loneliness. I can't be that girl anymore. But lately, it's like I'm there again, doing the same things all over. I don't like hiding how I truly feel and pretending to be okay with something that I'm not."

None of this was her fault. It was his. All his. "I'm sorry about tonight. I shouldn't have taken you like that. I saw you with Jake and everything went red. I lost my head."

She smiled sadly. "Damn. Guess I lied again."

He frowned, but before he could ask her what she meant, she said, "I told you I wanted a man to take control in the bedroom. Looks like what I really needed was a man to *lose* control. Don't apologize. It was hot. A perfect swan song."

He swallowed heavily. "No." He stood quickly, but Leah was too fast, too dressed. She was at the top of the ladder before he had his jeans in his hands.

"Leah, wait."

She paused after climbing on to the top rung. "I can't do this anymore. I'm sorry. Goodbye, Sawyer."

She descended as he rushed to pull on his jeans, calling out her name as she continued to walk out of the barn. By the time, he made it to the driveway, her taillights were all he could see as she drove away. He stood by the door of the barn for a long time, JD's words haunting him. *Some girls will leave you wanting more than a tumble in the hayloft.*

Leah was that girl. She made him want everything.

He stared off into the distance, then headed toward the house, clenching his T-shirt in his hands. He was barefoot, but he didn't care. He didn't intend to rejoin the party. He was going upstairs to figure out where the hell things had gone so wrong.

"Damn. That's a heavy look for a celebration."

Sawyer had been so preoccupied he hadn't seen JD sitting on the front porch.

"What are you doing out here?"

JD leaned against the cushions of the rocking chair and sighed. "I watched the party for a bit until your mother and Lucy ganged up on me and put me in bed. I couldn't sleep, so I snuck out here for some fresh air. Thought I'd enjoy the moonlight."

Sawyer put his shirt on, then glanced at the sky. "It's a bright one tonight."

"Where have you been? I figure Beth's back there right now, looking for a dance partner."

Sawyer grinned at JD's small dig. His father had jokingly referred to Beth as *the stalker* when Sawyer dated her in high school. Teased him mercilessly for her fervent, almost manic devotion to him. "I snuck away with Leah."

JD nodded, gently swaying in the rocking chair, his walker beside him like a silent guardian, reminding Sawyer of exactly how much his life was changing.

"Yeah, I figured as much by her hasty escape and your lack of clothing. 'Bout damn time you and little Leah Hollister finally managed to open your eyes and find each other."

Sawyer claimed the porch swing. "What's that supposed to mean? As I recall, it was you who talked me out of asking her to senior prom."

JD chuckled. "Son. Your mother constantly tells you how much you're like me. Have you ever thought about what that means?"

Sawyer shrugged. "I figured out it's not a compliment. She usually says that at the same time she's yelling at me for being a cocky ass."

JD took a handkerchief from his pocket and ran it over his face. It wasn't a particularly warm evening, but Sawyer could see the sheen of sweat on his father's brow. "Yeah. That's about right. Vicky's always accused me of having too much of that particular trait myself. I like to tell her she's confusing cockiness for confidence."

Sawyer nodded. "That's a good line. I'll have to remember that."

JD shrugged. "I have my moments. Not that it ever fooled your mother. Thing is, when you were in school, you had too much of that damn confidence. You strutted around like you were a football god and a stud with the girls."

Sawyer wished he could deny it, but his father nailed him pretty good. "Yeah. Guess I did. Don't know what that has to do with me taking Leah to prom though."

"You were a week away from graduating and two months from joining the Coast Guard. Only thing on your mind at that time was getting laid. There were plenty of other girls sniffing around you to scratch that itch, Beth standing at the front of the line."

"Why not Leah?"

JD shook his head. "Every time that girl came around here, you grew up."

Sawyer frowned. "What do you mean?"

"The cockiness disappeared. You stopped strutting and became real. It was the only time I got a good glimpse of the man you were going to be."

Sawyer swallowed heavily. "I didn't realize that."

"Of course you didn't. You were pretty stupid in those days."

They laughed, but the action caught up to JD, who started coughing roughly. The sound ripped at Sawyer's guts. "You want some water?"

JD shook his head, taking several deep, relieved breaths when the spell passed. "No. I'm okay now."

They sat in silence for several moments and Sawyer's mind raced over all the things he wanted to say to his father. His whole life he'd looked up to JD, aspired to be him when he grew up. He'd never idolized athletes or rock stars, never wanted anything more than to be a man his father would be proud of.

He recalled what Sam said about the wedding making JD stronger. "I think I'm in love with her, JD."

His father pierced him with a gaze that saw too much. "Maybe you're still a bit stupid after all."

Sawyer frowned. "What do you mean?"

"There's no *think* about it. You're head over heels for that girl and have been your whole life. You haven't told her that, have you?"

Sawyer shook his head as he recalled how sad she'd looked when she left the hayloft. The only words he'd managed were *want* and *need*. He'd given her no glimpse of what was truly in his heart. "No."

"What's holding you back?"

Sawyer leaned forward, placed his elbows on his knees, trying to find a way to explain. "It's not exactly a good time, JD."

His father snorted. "Bullshit. Don't you dare blame your cowardice on my illness. Whether I'm alive or dead, it makes no difference in the way you feel about that girl."

"I don't have a job, JD. I'm floundering around here on this ranch with no goals, no idea what my future holds."

"Sam said he told you about the sheriff position."

Sawyer nodded. "He did."

"Seemed to think you might be interested in it."

Sawyer ran a hand through his hair. "Yeah. I think that might be something I'd like to try."

"Guess the real question is if you plan to stick around. Did you come home for the right reasons?"

"What's that supposed to mean?"

"Son, if you don't want to live in Compton Pass, if you miss that ocean of yours, now is the time to say so. Coming home for me or for Leah is a piss-poor excuse. If this place doesn't call to you, if it isn't going to make you happy, then you need to get your ass on a plane and head back to the coast."

Sawyer shook his head. "I'm staying. I belong here."

JD rubbed his chin. "You know, Compton Pass doesn't exactly offer some of the more specialized distractions you probably enjoyed in the bigger cities."

It was the closest JD had ever come to asking him outright about his sexual proclivities. "You'd be surprised."

162

JD grinned. "No. I don't think I would. So I guess it boils down to you getting your head out of your ass and telling that girl what's in your heart."

Sawyer laughed. "Christ, you're the second person to mention my head-in-ass affliction."

"I'm glad you're home, Sawyer."

Sawyer swallowed heavily. The lump that had started to form with Leah's hasty departure tripled in size. "I am too, Pa."

"Sawyer," his father said quietly.

"Yeah?"

"I'm going to need some help getting to bed." JD avoided his gaze.

Sawyer gently lifted his father from the rocking chair. He supported most of JD's weight as they made the slow trek down the hall to his parents' bedroom. He tucked his father into bed. Then Sawyer claimed the seat Lucy had moved in earlier in the week, so JD could receive visitors.

The two of them sat in silence for a nearly an hour, listening to the light strains of music drifting from the backyard. Eventually JD accompanied it with soft snoring. For days, Sawyer had struggled to say the things he needed to tell his father. He realized sometimes words weren't necessary.

Peace seeped into his bones and the world finally clicked into place.

He was home.

His family would be fine.

He loved Leah.

Chapter Nine

Sawyer looked out at the bright morning sunshine. It was a great day for a wedding. He stretched and rubbed his neck, a groan crossing his lips.

"That doesn't sound good."

He turned as Silas and Colby joined him on the side porch. He'd come out for fresh air and to hide from his mother, who was on a rampage, worrying about a bunch of shit that didn't matter as far as he could tell. She'd spent half the morning fretting over the fact the yellow flowers were too large for the bouquets.

"Yeah, well, blame it on our brothers. I lugged tables and chairs from the barn all day yesterday for that rehearsal dinner only to have to drag them into some different configuration this morning for the wedding. I'm fucking cooked."

Colby slapped him on the back. "I feel your pain, bro. Lucy and Vicky have had me towing so much shit around this week, I'm afraid I'm going to start braying like a pack mule."

Sawyer chuckled, but Silas never cracked a smile. "Wish I'd been able to help more."

Colby rolled his eyes. "Please. I figure Saw and I got off easy. Noticed Lucy had you decorating cookies last night."

"No way." Sawyer laughed. "Hot damn. Looks like Karma got you after all. That's what you get for not calling me about JD."

Silas scowled and pointed his finger at Colby. "First of all, you weren't supposed to fucking say anything about the cookies and secondly,—" he looked at Sawyer, "—what the hell are you talking about? Karma? What kind of hippie bullshit is that? You didn't join up with one of those cult things in San Francisco, did you?"

Sawyer shook his head, grinning. "Nope. I'm cult-free. Promise."

Silas sighed, then grabbed a nearby chair to sit. He rubbed his thigh, wincing. When Si thought no one was looking, Sawyer had caught his brother doing more strenuous work than he should to help with the wedding preparations. Silas had taken great care to hide that fact from Lucy and Colby, so Sawyer didn't call him out for it. He understood pride far too well.

Silas studied him for a long time. "It's good to be here together. I know the rest of us have been on the ranch for a while, but it didn't start to feel like home again until you stepped out of that car two weeks ago."

Sawyer grinned. "Is that you're way of saying you missed me?"

"Jesus. You and Colby are fucking killing me today. Damn wedding is making everybody act like pansy-asses."

"Sorry. I'll try to limit the rest of my interactions with you today to belching and off-color jokes."

Si punched him lightly on the shoulder. "That's all I ask."

"There you guys are." Lucy rushed into the room. "Colby, Si, do you guys mind touching base with the bartender Vicky hired? Apparently he's having trouble with the keg and that doo-hickey that goes on top of it."

"Some bartender," Silas grumbled, rising slowly. "Can't even tap a damn keg."

Sawyer hated seeing his brother struggling to get around,

but he was grateful to have him here when he considered how close Si had come to losing his life in the oil-rig accident. Silas's friend, Red, hadn't been so lucky.

Colby and Silas followed Lucy out, leaving Sawyer alone again. He leaned on the railing and sighed. It was peaceful on this side of the house. For a moment, he could pretend there weren't nearly a hundred folks—friends and family—gathering in the backyard.

Sawyer turned when he heard a wolf whistle coming from the door. He grinned when he spotted Leah checking him out. She'd come to find him. That fact gave him hope.

She was smiling at him, though her eyes betrayed her nervousness. "Dayum. You clean up real good, cowboy."

His gaze took in her pastel-green sundress. "I don't hold a candle to you. You look incredible."

She propped her guitar against a wall. "You ready for your big walk down the aisle?"

Sawyer shook his head. "Jesus. I can't believe I let Cindi and Jody talk me into this."

"Viral wedding marches are all the rage these days. Don't you watch YouTube?"

"I like to limit my Internet usage to porn and fantasy football."

"Ah," she said. "Nice to know you're focused on the really important things."

He shrugged. "It's a talent." She stepped closer and he couldn't resist touching her. He ran his fingers through her hair, glad she'd opted to leave it down. "You ready for your song?"

"Yep. Been practicing for days. I'm pretty sure if I never hear it again, it'll be too soon."

"Can't wait to hear you sing. Listen, Leah. Can we talk?"

She adjusted the bowtie on his tuxedo and gave him an anxious smile. "Yeah. I think we should. I was wrong to run off last night without giving you a chance to respond. I let my fear get the better of me."

He fought to keep his cock from responding to her hands on him. The wedding march was going to be painful enough without trying to hide a hard-on at the same time. "What were you afraid of?"

"Rejection. I figured you couldn't tell me to get lost if I wasn't there to hear it. JD yanked me aside just now and gave me an earful for it."

"He did?"

"He told me the Leah he knew didn't run from anything, and he fully expected me to stand my ground and hear you out before this day was through. He really gave it to me." She smiled. His father's chastisement hadn't truly upset her. "For the first time in my life, I sort of felt what it's like to have a father."

Her voice broke slightly.

Sawyer's heart twinged at her admission. "You called him JD."

She laughed, though there was a definite sheen of tears in her eyes. "He made me say it to his face again. Three times."

Sawyer cupped her cheek. "I'm glad the old man is reverting to character and interfering. Used to drive me nuts in high school, but today—"

"Sawyer? Leah?" Vicky peeked her head out of the house. "You ready? We're about to start."

Sawyer sighed. He'd been a fool to try to have this conversation now. "Guess so."

Leah gave him a tense glance, then a quick kiss on the cheek. "Finish this after the wedding?"

He nodded.

She looked like she had more to say, but couldn't with Vicky watching them. She wrung her hands nervously. Clearly she was expecting the worse. She turned to leave.

"Hey, wait." To heck with his mom. He took Leah's hand and drew her toward him. He kissed her, trying hard to infuse it with as much passion as possible. "This isn't going to be a bad talk," he whispered. "Promise."

Sawyer caught a glimpse of his mother's beaming face. Vicky obviously didn't object to her son's public show of affection. He would be subjected to the third degree from her later. He figured the only thing holding her back the last few days had been the wedding plans.

Leah's smile returned, her face clearing. "Okay. See you at the altar."

She picked up her guitar and followed Vicky into the house. Sawyer stared after her, feeling like a lovesick fool, wishing they were meeting at the altar for a different reason, a much more romantic one.

Sam appeared at the door. "There you are. You ready?"

Sawyer nodded.

"You have the ring?"

He pulled Cindi's wedding band out of his pocket. "I've got it covered, bro. No worries."

"Great. Thanks." Sam walked out on the porch and tugged at the shirtsleeves beneath his Brioni tuxedo. His brother may be back in the country, but something told Sawyer they'd never break Sam of all his citified ways and expensive tastes. "I can't believe how fast all of this is happening. Three months ago I was in New York, working my ass off for a promotion and trying to hook up with a woman in the office. Didn't even know Cindi."

"And now you're about to pledge your life to her." Sawyer jerked his thumb toward the driveway. "You know, that Maserati Granturismo of yours would make a pretty good get-away car. Nobody would catch us in that thing. Hell, I'd even be willing to take one for the team and drive."

Sam laughed. "Yeah. Why do I get the feeling your suggestion isn't to save me as much as to get behind the wheel of my baby?"

Sawyer faked a disappointed face. "That hurts, man. Here I am offering to save you and you accuse me of car envy. Besides, we'd look pretty ridiculous huddling together on Jenn's back."

"I'm not going anywhere." Sam spoke with conviction.

"I know. Cindi's perfect for you. I'm glad you found someone to make you happy."

Sam smiled. "I've been pretty preoccupied with the wedding and shit, but as soon as Cindi and I come home from the honeymoon I think you and I should have a talk about Leah. I'm not sure you're seeing the big picture with her."

Sawyer grinned. "Actually, I had my eyes opened for me last night."

"Who do I have to thank for that?"

"JD *and* Leah. I've been acting like a fool."

Sam placed a hand on his shoulder. "You can say that again. Although, the idea of you hooking up with a kindergarten teacher strikes me as pretty funny. You think she can do anything about your inability to spell? Better yet, she can tie your shoes for you."

Sawyer reached up and mussed Sam's hair.

"Dammit, Saw." Sam tried to finger comb it in place. "Have

a little respect for the groom."

"Hey." Seth came into the room. "Leah took her seat by the altar. Think the music's getting ready to start." He patted Sam on the shoulder. "How you holding up, man?"

"Fucking nervous. Why the hell did we let those women talk us into dancing down the aisle? I'm going to fall flat on my face. I know it."

"You weren't thinking with your brains on that one. That was definitely a cock call." Silas laughed as he rejoined them.

Sawyer agreed. "You're not kidding. You were the smart brother. Hooking up with a married couple to avoid all this wedding shit."

Silas grinned. "Never thought of that, but now that you mention it, guess I was pretty fucking clever. I left Colby to tap the keg. Figured you jokers would be hiding out. Found something at the bar to help." He pulled out a bottle of Crown Royal. Twisting off the cap, he passed it straight to Seth. Silas had quit drinking after his accident.

Sawyer looked at Si. "Don't know why you're laughing about the dancing. You have to do it too, you know?"

"Nobody's gonna laugh at a cripple trying to boogie."

Seth took a drink of the whiskey and handed it to Sam. "Jody's going to kill me when she smells that on my breath."

Sam tipped up the bottle. "If they insist on us doing that damn silly wedding march, they're going to have to make some allowances for nerves." Wiping his mouth with the back of his hand, he handed the bottle to Sawyer.

Sawyer took his turn, enjoying the heat of the liquor as it slid down his throat. "Damn. That's good stuff."

"Hell's bells, boys. You gonna stand around yammering all day or you gonna get married?" JD shuffled into the room, leaning heavily on his walker. Sawyer heard Vicky say his father was determined not to use it for the wedding march and they were all a bit worried about him falling.

Sawyer tried to hide the liquor behind his back, but he wasn't quick enough.

"What do you have there? Crown Royal? Thank God. I knew I raised you boys right. Pass that over."

Sawyer grinned as his father lifted the whiskey to them. "To the Compass brothers. Long may they reign."

JD took a drink before handing it to Silas. "Better cap that up before your mother catches us. Look sharp. It's time."

They all followed JD to the backyard.

Once they were in place at the back of the crowd, Sawyer caught Leah's eye and winked. She was seated near the arbor that would serve as an altar. She smiled, and then played the opening chords of the song Jody and Cindi had selected for their wedding march. The bouncy rhythm of Colbie Callait's *I Do* started. Leah's singing was as sweet as the song.

Colby stepped forward first. To the delight of everyone in the crowd he danced Vicky down the aisle, twirling her twice before he led her to her seat in the front row. The ranch hands clapped, hooted and hollered when Lucy and Silas followed, Lucy doing some fancy footwork, while Silas added a bit more bounce to his limp and spun his cane like a baton.

Sawyer stood next to Paul, Jody's unusual choice for her maid of honor. Sawyer tipped his hat at Leah before making his way to the altar. He was pretty proud of his fancy Texas two-step until the New Yorker, Paul, dropped down on the ground and break-danced. The crowd went wild when Sawyer helped Paul to his feet and they took their places.

Sawyer laughed as Seth and Sam did a crazy do-si-do together. They stood together by the altar as the crowd strained

171

for a glimpse of Thomas jitterbugging his daughter Jody to the front.

Sawyer glanced at Seth and grinned at the look of pure joy on his brother's face. Seth met them at the altar as Thomas spun Jody into his brother's arms. Everyone cheered, then turned around for the last pairing.

Leah slowed the song down when JD stepped forward with Cindi on his arm, looking prouder than Sawyer had ever seen him. Cindi had come to Compass ranch, a lonely young woman looking for a home. JD and Vicky had taken her into their fold and loved her as much as they would have had she been their true daughter.

Sawyer caught Vicky wiping her eyes as JD waltzed with Cindi. JD made it with grace and for the first time in his life, Sawyer knew what true strength was.

When they reached the front, JD put her hand in Sam's, covering their grasp with his own. "Be good to each other," he said loud enough for all of them standing by the altar to hear. Sawyer suspected JD meant his encouragement for the entire wedding party.

Sawyer tried to swallow the lump in his throat as he memorized his father's face at that moment—certain he'd never seen JD look happier.

JD took his seat next to Vicky and the vows were exchanged. When the minister told his brothers to kiss their brides, Sawyer snuck a peek at Leah.

She was smiling, though there were tears streaming down her face. He caught her gaze and held it.

"I love you," Sawyer mouthed.

She blinked and twisted her head. He'd shocked her. Her forehead crinkled as she tried to figure out if he'd really said what she thought.

Unfortunately, the minister stopped him from repeating the sentiment, announcing the two new Mr. and Mrs. Comptons. Leah quickly repositioned her guitar on her lap and began playing the recessional music. Sawyer was quickly shanghaied by his mother for pictures.

It was nearly an hour before he managed to catch up to Leah again. Jody and Cindi—bless their souls—had seated them next to each other at one of the front tables.

"Hey," she said as he took his chair. "That wedding was amazing."

He agreed. "You nailed the song. Perfect."

She smiled. "Yeah, well, it was pretty easy to sing considering no one was looking at me. You should have seen your face when Paul started spinning on his head. Priceless."

Sawyer laughed. "Didn't realize the guy was so damn competitive. We made a little wager over dinner last night. I mentioned the fact I did a pretty mean Texas two-step. He said my country-bumpkin moves would pale in comparison to the skills he had. Next thing you know, we're trash-talking and making a damn bet on who'd be the best."

"Ouch. What was the wager?"

Sawyer glanced at his watch. "In about three hours, I'm going to be out there in the middle of that dance floor break-dancing to Michael Jackson's *Billie Jean*. If I'd won, we would have been treated to Paul two-stepping to *Friends in Low Places*. Might still make the son of a bitch do that anyway."

Leah cracked up. "Thank God I remembered to bring my camera."

He leaned closer and kissed her, taking a deep whiff of her floral perfume. She smelled like roses.

Before he could repeat the words he'd mouthed during the

service, Silas, Lucy and Colby joined them. The caterers began delivering their food. JD and Vicky sat with them as well, while Jody, Seth, Cindi and Sam shared a smaller table nearby at the front of the makeshift dance floor.

"Damn, that was a great wedding," JD said.

"It was," Vicky concurred, her smile so big Sawyer wondered if it hurt her face.

"You did good, darlin'," JD added, lifting his mother's hand and kissing it.

"Oh, shoot. I didn't do that much. Those girls knew what they wanted."

Lucy pointed her fork at Vicky. "And you made it happen. Don't you dare try to downplay your role in this party."

JD nodded approvingly. "You tell her, sweet Lu."

Lucy, a nurse, had taken over most of the care JD required, keeping tabs on his medicine and helping him through the rough spells. She'd been a godsend, and Sawyer made a mental note to draw her aside tonight and tell her so.

The conversation during dinner was light and fun as everyone recalled their favorite part of the ceremony. Leah blushed when Colby told her he preferred her version of the wedding-march song to the one played on the radio.

After the dishes were cleared, the deejay started the music, playing the special songs Jody and Cindi had selected for the dances with the parents. Vicky got two as she danced first with Seth and then with Sam.

When the deejay finally invited everyone to the floor, Sawyer grasped Leah's hand. "Dance with me."

She accepted his invitation and he dragged her close as they swayed to the soft strains of Garth Brooks singing *To Make You Feel My Love*. The instant Sawyer heard Leah humming along, he knew they'd found their song.

She pressed her face against his. "Sawyer, at the end of the ceremony, you said something—"

He grinned. "I love you."

She looked at him. "You do?"

"Very much. You left last night before I could tell you. I've been an idiot, Leah."

She shook her head. "No, you haven't. Everything's happening so fast."

"I know that. Hell, I'm struggling to see anything clearly, but when I go to bed every night, the only thing I know for certain is that when I wake up, I need you there."

"I want to be there."

Sawyer picked her up and twirled her around. "Good. And so I'm sure we've got this straight, you're my girlfriend. You're not my fuck-buddy, my friend with benefits, my distraction. You're my future, my love, my rose."

"I love you too, Sawyer."

"What do you say we get out of here and do a little private celebrating?"

"Now?" she asked, giving him an exasperated look.

He glanced around. The dance floor was packed as his entire family settled in, ready to enjoy themselves until the wee hours. "No one will even notice we're gone."

She rolled her eyes. "Everyone will miss you. You have a toast to propose, Mr. Best Man."

"Damn. I forgot about that."

"No, you didn't. Besides I know what you're really trying to do, and I'm not going to help you."

"What's that?"

"You are not reneging on your break-dancing bet."

He groaned. "Please?"

She kissed him softly. "No way. I'm living for it. There's no rush, Saw. We have all the time in the world."

She was right. They did.

Chapter Ten

It was so late, it was early when Leah finally escaped the wedding reception with Sawyer.

"What time is it?" she asked.

Sawyer glanced at his watch. "After two a.m."

"Wow. That was an amazing party."

He grinned over his shoulder, but continued to lead her away from the house and deeper into the woods.

"Where are we going?"

"You'll see." He took the path slowly so she wouldn't trip. Sawyer had disappeared with Jake and a few of the ranch hands around midnight. They'd been gone nearly half an hour. Sawyer said they'd smoked cigars behind the barn. Problem was Leah had noticed a distinct lack of cigar smell on his clothing and breath.

She heard the trickle of the creek that ran through Compass ranch. She, Sawyer and Sam had come here more than a few times when they were young to fish, skip rocks and generally wallow away a lazy summer afternoon.

As they approached, a soft light appeared. "What's that?"

"We're here," Sawyer said.

Leah stepped into the clearing by the creek and gasped.

A canopy bed was set up, complete with sheets, a comforter and pillows. Off to the side a camp lantern burned, casting the entire area in romantic lighting. It was the most beautiful thing Leah had ever seen.

"I used a net instead of the real canopy. Figured that would keep the bugs away. And that's a thick quilt, so even if it gets chilly, I think we'll be okay."

"You did this? For me?"

Sawyer grasped her hand tighter. "Leah, I would do anything for you."

She closed her eyes to ward of the happy tears threatening to fall. "How—"

"Recruited Jake and a few of the hands. Remembered the old bed was in the storage building behind the barn. Only took us a couple trips to get it all here and assembled. Vicky snuck out after we left to put on the sheets and such."

Leah blushed. "Your mother helped?"

Sawyer laughed. "She actually yelled at me for not giving her more notice. She said she could've had the place looking really nice if she'd known what I was up to ahead of time."

Leah took in the scene. "There's no way to make this any nicer. It's perfect."

Sawyer led her to the bed. "I figured neither one of us was in any condition to drive to your place after all the champagne we drank. And given how you scream down the rafters in bed, I wouldn't have been able to do everything I planned to do to you without keeping everyone awake."

Leah punched him lightly. "I don't scream."

He wiggled his eyebrows. "You would have tonight."

"Cocky ass."

Sawyer shook his head and gave her a mischievous grin. "You're mistaking confidence for cockiness."

She snorted. "No. I'm not."

Sawyer kissed her hard, his lips devouring hers. "I love you, Leah."

178

After that, they didn't speak. Instead, they conveyed their feelings with touches, kisses, caresses. They undressed each other leisurely, taking their time as they unveiled each bit of bare flesh.

Sawyer played with her breasts for so long, she thought she might climax from that alone. When she pushed his tuxedo pants down, she followed the material, worshipping Sawyer's erection with her mouth, licking, nipping, sucking on the hard flesh. Once she'd had her fill, she moved to his back, tracing every line of his tattoo with her tongue.

"Wait a minute. Your tattoo."

"What about it?"

"There's a rose growing out of the ranch brand."

Sawyer glanced over his shoulder at her and smiled. "Wondered when you'd notice that. Put you there when I was eighteen. I might have been going west, but I knew where my true home was."

A tear ran down her cheek, amazement and joy radiating from her face. "The rose is for me?"

"You've always been special, different. Unfortunately, I had a lot of growing up to do."

"Oh, don't be silly. You still have a lot of growing up to do," she teased.

Sawyer laughed. "Oh, baby, you're going to pay for that one."

"You can punish me later," she whispered.

Dropping to her knees, she bit his ass cheeks, soothing away the sting with soft kisses. Sawyer groaned. "God dammit, rose," he said, through gritted teeth when she sucked one of her fingers into her mouth, wetting it before toying with his anus. He jolted like he'd been struck by lightning, but he didn't move away.

"Don't get too fond of that game," he warned.

She laughed and pressed in to the second knuckle. She wiggled it a bit as Sawyer clenched his fists by his sides.

"More?" she asked.

He shook his head. "Christ. Not tonight, Leah. I'm going to need some time to decide if I love or hate that."

She withdrew her finger slowly, grinning at his response. He was trying to make the evening special for her, stepping out of his comfort zone along the way. "Thank you for letting me play." Her dominant lover was showing great restraint. She appreciated his efforts in the face of her unbelievable happiness. She wanted to touch every inch of him, mark him as hers. He seemed to understand, and he gave her free rein to satisfy the need.

When Sawyer separated the canopy net, Leah climbed onto the plush comforter, her hand brushing something soft. Rose petals. The entire bed was covered in beautiful red petals.

She looked at Sawyer, smiling widely.

"That was my idea."

"Thank you," she whispered. No one had ever gone to such lengths for her. Given her such an incredible gift. She was moved beyond words.

She lifted her arms, inviting Sawyer to join her. He crawled onto the bed, gripping her waist and pulling her beneath him on the center of the mattress.

Their kisses seemed to last for hours, neither of them willing to give up the comfort, the beauty of this moment.

Sawyer slid slowly along her body, planting kisses on her neck, her breasts, her stomach. He touched every inch of her sensitive skin. When his lips grazed her clit, she opened her legs, crying out at his much-more-intimate kiss.

As his tongue darted in and out of her opening, Leah realized he'd been right to take them away from the house. She couldn't have held in her cries of delight, her pleas for more.

When Sawyer pressed two fingers into her pussy, she saw heaven, splintering into white-hot bliss as her orgasm came. She ran her fingers through Sawyer's hair, trying to use her grip to drag his face up to hers.

"Come inside me."

He shook his head. "Not yet, Leah. I'll tell you when."

He reached toward the bottom of the bed. For the first time, she noticed the small basket there.

"What's that?"

"Supplies."

He collected a tube of lubrication and a slim vibrator. Leah recalled that his mother had been here and she frowned.

"I brought this out after Vicky worked her magic with the rose petals."

"How did you know—"

He shrugged. "I'm finding it easier and easier to read your expressions, your thoughts."

She smiled wickedly. "Can you tell what I'm thinking now?"

He nodded. "Hell yeah." He shoved two fingers inside her. "You want to come again."

Her eyes drifted closed as he thrust into her ultra-sensitive pussy. "God, Saw. So good." She was on the verge of exploding when he retreated. "Wait. Don't stop."

He shook his head. "No, you've already gotten a freebie. Now you're going to wait for permission."

He opened the tube of lubrication and spread a generous

amount on his finger. She started to tell him that wasn't going to be necessary. The juices of her arousal coated her thighs. She was plenty wet enough to take him in.

His finger brushed against her ass and she realized his intent. "Payback?" she asked, the word coming out on a harsh breath.

"Lift your legs."

She bent her knees, allowing Sawyer better access to her ass as he grabbed an extra pillow and placed it beneath her hips.

"Jake offered to join us tonight."

His comment caught her unaware. "What?"

"When we were setting up the bed, Jake said he'd be willing to play the third if we had a hankering to indulge in a threesome."

Leah's head swam with the idea. "A ménage?"

He nodded. "You ever tried that?"

She shook her head. "No. Have you?"

His face told her instantly that he had. "A couple of times at BDSM parties. Another Dom asked me to play the third in a scene between him and his sub. She liked being taken by two men."

Leah's mouth suddenly went dry. "At the same time?"

He chuckled. "Don't look so horrified. It is possible, you know? Some women really get off on it."

Leah tried to figure out if she was that kind of woman. Lucy was radiantly happy in her committed threesome with Silas and Colby. Even Cindi had confided to her a certain kink for multiple partners. Leah wondered what it would be like, but she didn't feel the same pull toward that practice as she did the bondage, the pain.

"Did you like it?" she asked.

He placed his hand on her thigh, gently caressing her skin. "It was okay. I was the extra guy, so for me, it was strictly sex."

Sawyer looked at her. "Leah, I meant it when I said I'd give you anything. If you want to explore a ménage, I'll do it."

She took a deep breath and spoke the truth, praying it wouldn't drive Sawyer away. "I don't want to."

He released a long, relieved breath. "Thank God. I told Jake we'd consider it, but if you'd said yes and he'd come to this bed, I'm terrified I would have killed him the second he touched you. I realized the other night I'm a jealous bastard. Men get near you and I lose my head."

She laughed. "I share that trait. I got detention for skipping gym because it was either that or beat the crap out of Beth for bragging about doing *it* with you."

"Gotta admit I'm disappointed to hear that. A catfight between you and Beth would be pretty—"

Leah pinched Sawyer's thigh hard. "Don't finish that statement."

Sawyer grinned, looking far from chastised. "I never saw jealousy as a particularly hot feature in a woman, but it looks pretty damn good on you."

Sawyer's finger pressed harder against Leah's tight hole, and the conversation died. She closed her eyes, trying to ward off the climax threatening to erupt when he worked first one, then two fingers into her ass.

"Does that hurt?" he asked.

"Yes," she hissed. "I fucking love it."

He chuckled and continued thrusting. "Thought we might find some creative ways to have a threesome with just the two of us."

He removed his fingers, returning almost immediately with the vibrator.

She gasped when he slowly pushed the slim toy into her rear. "Ohmigod," she cried, when he turned it on low.

She expected—hoped—he'd fuck her now. Her pussy was empty and she was overwhelmed by the need for him to fill her.

"Come for me, rose." He teased her to a second hard orgasm.

"Sawyer, please," she begged. "Come inside me."

"Not yet."

He played with her forever, leading her to climax after climax with his tongue, his teeth, his fingers. She thrashed against the mattress in a mindless haze of endless ecstasy.

Finally, exhausted, sated out of her mind, she panted, "Can't. Take. Any more."

Sawyer raised his head, looked up at the sky and said, "One more."

Leah followed his gaze and saw the sun rising on the horizon as Sawyer turned the vibrator in her ass on high and thrust his cock into her body. She exploded, splintered, shattered.

And, as he predicted, she screamed.

Chapter Eleven

The phone rang, jarring Sawyer from a deep, contented sleep. He looked around the room, taking a moment to remember where he was—Leah's apartment. He glanced down and discovered Leah snug within his arms. They'd worn each other out last night, making love until the wee hours of the morning.

In the month since the wedding, he'd spent more nights at Leah's apartment than he had at the ranch. Leah was uncomfortable spending the night in his bed, claiming it was disrespectful to his parents. He loved her old-fashioned values and how staunchly she stuck to them.

Sawyer still continued to eat dinner with his family every night, Leah often joining them at the table. Afterwards, they'd adjourn to the living room to watch movies or play games. While Sawyer knew the entire family was trying to hoard every moment they could with their father, he'd enjoyed reconnecting with his brothers as well. They spent hours catching up on the years apart and, in some ways, it was like they'd never left Compass ranch at all.

Vicky and JD always invited Leah to stay, but she'd refuse with a blush. Sawyer would drive her home and they'd spend the night doing a little reuniting of their own. The friendship they'd always shared blossomed and their love deepened more with each passing day.

Sawyer picked up his phone. "Hello?"

"Saw. I think you should come home."

His heart stopped when he heard Sam's urgent tone.

"JD?"

Sam cleared his throat, trying to mask the agony in his tone. "Yeah. It's not good. It was a rough night. I don't think any of us expected this to happen so fast."

"JD's lived longer than the doctor said he would. I think there's a difference between expectations and hope."

Sam sighed. "Guess you're right."

Sawyer closed his eyes in regret. He should have stayed home last night. His gut instinct had told him to remain, but he'd let JD convince him he was okay, telling him to go and have fun.

Sam interrupted his thoughts. "He's asking to see Leah too."

"We'll be right there."

Leah lifted her head, concern rife on her face. "Sawyer? What is it?"

"We have to go."

She rose quickly, dressing in the jeans he'd peeled off her the previous night. They both dressed in silence, but before he could put on his boots, he stilled. "I'm not sure I can do this, Leah."

She'd grabbed a clean T-shirt from her dresser and donned it. Her face was filled with understanding. "You're one of the strongest men I've ever known, Saw. You have to keep putting one foot in front of the other."

He rubbed his forehead wearily. "Right. Okay." His body was numb with dread. "You ready to go?"

She took his hand. "Yeah. I am."

They drove to the ranch in silence and Sawyer tried to mentally prepare himself to face this day. JD's health had declined steadily in the month following the wedding. Last week, he'd stopped getting out of bed, his body finally wearing out. They'd all tried to put on a good face, moving their games and movies to JD's bedroom, pretending like they didn't see what was coming.

The hardest part about all of it was watching JD suffer. His spirit was stronger than ever. Sawyer couldn't imagine what it was like for his father to lay in a bed, helpless, while his mind was still fully aware and cognizant of everything going on around him.

When they arrived at the ranch, Sawyer was surprised to find his brothers sitting in the living room rather than with JD. Seth and Sam had both postponed their honeymoons when JD took a fall the morning after the wedding. It had scared the shit out of them at the time. Now, when Sawyer looked back on it, all he could recall was how downright healthy his father had looked in comparison to now.

His mother entered the room, carrying a tray loaded with bagels and muffins. Sawyer took it from her, placing it on the coffee table. The more JD's health declined, the more energetic Vicky became. She'd been in perpetual motion since Sawyer arrived home. At first, he'd thought it was because of the wedding, but now he realized his mother was coping with her grief through constant activity. He was terrified of the moment when she stopped moving.

"What's up?" he asked.

Silas jerked his finger toward the hall. "Lucy shooed us out. Said our constant hovering was grating on *her* nerves, so she could only imagine how JD felt."

Sawyer took one glance at the anxious faces surrounding him and appreciated Lucy's concern. "I might peek in for a minute."

Silas looked like he'd object, so Sawyer darted out of the living room. He'd tried to brace himself during the car trip for what he'd be faced with, and he thought he'd better do it now before he lost his nerve.

At the end of the hall, he paused. He could hear Lucy's voice. Peering in, he found his sister-in-law perched on the side of JD's bed. She had his hand in hers, both pressed to her belly, and they were crying softly. Sawyer stood motionless, unable to lower his gaze despite the fact he'd obviously stepped into a personal conversation.

"Silas is hoping for a boy, of course. I think the idea of having a daughter terrifies him."

JD smiled weakly. "I got lucky. Dodged that bullet with my boys. What's Colby say?"

Lucy grinned. "Oh, you know Colby. So long as the baby is healthy and happy, he's doesn't care either way."

Lucy was pregnant? Sawyer smiled despite the agony tearing through his gut.

"I wish I was going to be here to see the littlest Compton, Lu. You tell that baby Grandpa JD loved him...or her...more than anything."

Lucy sniffled, wiping her nose with the back of her hand. Her voice trembled when she promised, "I will."

"You're going to be a wonderful mother, Lucy."

His reassurance broke the last of Lucy's restraint and she bent forward, quietly crying against JD's chest. Sawyer's father stroked her hair gently, promising her everything would be okay.

Sawyer stepped into the hall, careful to keep his presence unknown. He only made it two steps from the door when his strength failed. Leaning against the wall, he slowly slid down until his ass hit the floor. He rested his head on his bent knees.

That was where Lucy found him several minutes later.

"Saw?" she whispered.

He looked up, unable to hide the tears streaming down his face. "Congratulations on the baby, Lucy."

She smiled sadly. "Thanks. JD's asking for you."

He took a deep breath and forced himself to stand. He recalled Leah's encouragement. *Put one foot in front of the other.*

He kept that advice in mind, practicing it until he found himself by his father's bed. "Hey, JD."

JD opened his eyes. "I already talked to the other boys this morning. Gonna tell you what I told them."

Sawyer nodded as he sat in the chair by the bed. "Okay."

"I want you to look after your mother. This is going to be hard on her for a while. Keep an eye on her."

"You don't need to ask that, Pa. We'll be here for her as long as she needs us."

JD coughed, the dry sound wracking his too-thin frame roughly.

"Be happy, Sawyer. You only get one shot at this life so don't screw it up. Find what makes you smile and hold onto it tight."

Leah's face drifted through his mind. "I think I can do that."

JD shook his head. "Boy, how many times do I have to tell you, there's no *think* to it? Lead with your heart. It won't steer you wrong."

"You're right. Leah makes me happy. I don't plan to let her go."

JD smiled weakly and nodded. "Good. 'Bout time you got

smart."

They both glanced up when they heard a knock at the door. Silas, Seth and Sam all stood there, shirtless.

It took a moment for Sawyer to understand what the devil they were up to. Rising, he pulled off his shirt as well.

JD looked at them, confused. "What—"

Silas stepped forward. "We've said a lot today, Pa. But you always taught us to be men of action. So there's something we have to show you. We hope you know how damn much we appreciate everything you've ever given us. Though we may have struck out on our own, you were never far from our hearts. You never will be."

One by one, each of them pivoted on their boot heels, allowing JD to see their tattoos for the first time. There wasn't a sound from the bed for a long time. Sawyer's heart raced as he wondered what their father thought of their secret tribute to Compass ranch and their parents. For each of them, it had been a way to carry home around with them as they took off to explore the world, to seek their destiny.

Sawyer recalled the first time he'd seen Silas's tattoo. He'd known—even at fifteen—that he'd have that same mark on his skin. He'd believed the tattoo would sustain him during the years he was gone. In many ways, it had.

But he'd been wrong to think he needed a visual reminder of Compass ranch. The tattoo was only skin-deep while his love for this land and his family went straight to the bone.

"These don't look new," JD said.

Silas turned around. "Nah. Mine's about ten years old. We got them on our eighteenth birthdays. Just before each of us left."

JD smiled and closed his eyes. "I should skin Snake alive."

They laughed, facing their father once more.

Vicky came in, gasping in surprise when she caught sight of their bare backs. "What the devil?"

She forced each of them to stand still as she traveled from son to son to son to son, studying each tattoo carefully, slowly. "You took us with you when you left."

Sawyer smiled when Sam embraced his mother gently.

"Everywhere," Sam whispered.

"And this..." Her eagle eyes surprised none of them. Vicky traced her initial entwining with JD's on Sawyer's back. "Think Snake will do one on me?"

"Don't need it, V." JD clipped his sentences, conserving energy. "We're permanent. Never forget."

"I swear it. And I have the only reminder I'll ever need." Vicky clung to Sam, silent tears falling. "My boys," she whispered.

JD coughed weakly. Vicky released her child, taking the chair by her husband's side. "What do you need, JD?"

He grasped her hand, his voice weak when he replied. "You, my love. That's all."

Vicky kissed his bony, gnarled fingers. Sawyer closed his eyes, choosing to remember the man his father had been before pancreatic cancer. Tall, strong, vibrant. That was the man imprinted on his heart, the one he was going to tell his nieces, nephews and children about.

JD's breathing became loud in the quiet room. The raspy sound drowned out even the pounding of Sawyer's heart.

"Seth. Get my girls. Colby, too. Wanna see everyone I love. Standing around me. Healthy. Happy. Alive. My legacy."

Seth slipped down the hall, returning in seconds, followed by the rest of the family. Leah strode straight toward Sawyer.

191

He was glad for her strength when she wrapped her arms around him. Even better, his brothers had the same support, the same love. Colby embraced Lucy as Silas came to stand behind Vicky, his hand resting on her shoulder.

None of them said a word as JD slowly scanned the room. When his gaze landed at last on Vicky, he smiled.

And closed his eyes.

Chapter Twelve

Two days later, Leah rocked on the front porch swing. She watched the sunrise with Sawyer and Vicky. The three of them sat together quietly, letting the morning sounds soothe them. The crickets were out in full-force, providing the soundtrack for the sky's show as the darkness faded to light, producing the most beautiful colors Leah had ever seen.

She'd stayed at the ranch with Sawyer since his father passed away. Once JD's body was taken from the house, the energy had drained out of Vicky like someone had pulled a plug. She had gone into the living room, claiming the couch, looking far too weary and refusing to budge. The family took turns keeping her company each day, while the others worked on taking care of all the preparations necessary for the funeral.

Vicky had offered some input, but for the most part, she was content to let them handle all the details. Each night, one of the boys would escort her to her bedroom and stay with her until she fell asleep. Leah's heart flooded with emotion when she saw the quiet care Vicky's sons gave to their mother.

Leah had woken up nearly an hour earlier when she heard Sawyer quietly moving around the bedroom. He'd told her to go back to sleep, but—like him—she couldn't stop thinking about the coming day.

JD's funeral was expected to be the largest Compton Pass had ever seen. A giant in the community, there wasn't a single soul in the area who didn't know and respect him. Rather than try to squeeze the entire town into the too-small funeral home, they'd opted to hold the ceremony on the ranch. Vicky had smiled when they'd proposed the idea, telling them JD would like that.

Leah and Sawyer had tiptoed downstairs together to discover Vicky had been the earlier bird. They'd enjoyed the quiet morning for nearly an hour without speaking, all of them lost in their thoughts.

Sawyer broke the silence first. "It's going to be a beautiful day."

Vicky nodded. "I bet JD's pulling some strings in heaven."

Leah liked the idea of JD providing the sunshine. The thought comforted her. "I think I smell bacon."

Vicky turned her head to the house. "That'll be Seth. It's his answer to all of life's problems."

Leah laughed. "Wow. Never considered that before, but I think he may be on to something."

"I'm hungry." It was the first time in two days Vicky had shown any appetite at all, never taking more than a bite or two when one of the boys insisted.

Sawyer stood up and grasped his mother's hand. "I'm starving. Let's go eat."

The morning passed slowly, no one in a hurry to move to the inevitable event. The whole family ate a leisurely breakfast, the conversation sparse and involving little more than someone asking for a plate to be passed. After breakfast, they retired to their separate spaces to get dressed. Sam and Cindi had their own little cottage on the property as did Lucy, Silas and Colby.

While nothing had been decided, Leah was certain Seth and Jody would remain at the ranch house with Vicky after the funeral. Sawyer had spent most of the past month dividing his time between home and Leah's apartment. They were still in the early days of their relationship, but she was hoping perhaps he'd move in with her once the dust settled.

The city council had offered him the sheriff's position a couple weeks earlier, so it made more sense for him to live closer to town. Roberts had agreed to stay on longer, training him on a part-time basis and allowing Sawyer the extra time to be with JD.

When a parade of cars started down the driveway, the family gathered together on the front porch. Sawyer handed Leah her guitar.

Once they arrived at the family's burial plot on the west side of the property, she would play. Though they'd expected a large crowd, Leah was amazed by the sheer number of people. It was as if every man, woman and child from Compton Pass was there. Her mother gave her a brief wave from the yard before dabbing her face with a tissue.

Leah's eyes filled with tears and she took a deep breath, forcing them away. She glanced at Sawyer, his face chiseled in stone. She suspected the veneer was starting to wear thin.

The night of JD's death, he'd crawled into his bed with her, put his head on her chest and quietly cried in her arms until he fell asleep. Since then, he'd taken up Vicky's habit of constant movement, handling most of the thousand little things that needed attending to and entertaining the steady stream of visitors to the ranch.

Silas appeared at the front door, holding the urn containing JD's ashes. Silas's usually impassive face was lined with pain. Leah lost her battle with tears. JD's oldest son would carry his father to his final resting place.

Sawyer wrapped his arm around her shoulder. "Moonshine jar," he whispered. "One of the few instructions JD left about what he'd like for his funeral."

Leah smiled through her tears. Only JD Compton would want to go to the great beyond in a moonshine jar.

Silas cradled the container, wrapped in JD's favorite flannel shirt, in his arm and started forward, leaning heavily on his cane. Colby helped Silas descend the porch stairs. On solid ground, Silas waited for his brothers to join him. The four Compass brothers led the procession as Vicky, wearing JD's cowboy hat, followed closely behind, supported by Colby. Leah walked with Lucy, Jody and Cindi.

The short trek to the cemetery plot was made without a sound, only the occasional sniffle breaking the silence. When they arrived, Leah saw the hole Colby had dug earlier in the day.

Glancing around, she observed the graves of earlier generations of Comptons, some of the stones dating to the early 1800s. She was overwhelmed by the sense of family, of tradition surrounding them. JD had been one in a long line of powerful, honorable men. Leah looked at Sawyer and recognized that same strength and pride in him.

Sawyer caught her gaze, and then nodded. She moved forward to sit on the chair Colby had provided for her. Opening her guitar case, she lifted the instrument to her lap and swallowed hard, forcing the lump in her throat away. JD had asked her to perform at his funeral. At the time, she would have promised him the moon.

Now she realized how difficult it was going to be to honor his request. He deserved a beautiful tribute, but her throat was tight with unshed tears. She closed her eyes and let the silence clear her mind. JD's smiling face appeared as she recalled him dancing Cindi down the aisle, giving her away to his son.

The image balanced her, gave her the power to sing. The opening strains of *Amazing Grace* were soft, but as she lost herself to the lyrics of the song, her voice gradually gained strength. She began to strum her guitar, singing louder. Colby joined her on the second verse and soon, everyone in the crowd added their voices to the melody.

As they sang, Silas uncapped the jar. Slowly, he poured his father's ashes into the hole. Once the container was empty, Vicky stepped forward. She took off JD's hat, placing it on top of the ashes.

Seth retrieved the shovel Colby had left near the gravesite, scooping up some of the loose earth and layering it in the hole. Then, he handed the tool to Sam, who followed suit.

Leah's voice wavered slightly when Sawyer accepted the shovel from his twin and added his own dirt to the grave. Sawyer wiped his face roughly as he passed it to Silas. Silas took his turn and then he approached his mother. Vicky put the last two mounds on JD's grave, tears streaming from her eyes.

She blew a kiss to JD, and then she stepped away. Seth was there, offering a strong hand at her back as the final strains of the song ended.

The four brothers stood by their mother, facing the crowd. Last night, they had met in the barn with a twelve-pack of beer—and two cans of Pepsi for Silas—to write their father's eulogy.

When he'd come to bed, well after midnight, Sawyer had reached for Leah in the darkness. She'd asked him how it had gone. Rather than answer, he'd pulled her beneath him, slowly pushing into her body. He'd trembled as he made love to her. She'd wrapped her arms around him, kissing away his silent tears.

Now the four brothers stood shoulder to shoulder. Someone handed Silas a microphone.

He cleared his throat. "Thank you all for coming today to the place my forefathers built. JD was the latest in a line of hardworking, generous and badass Comptons. I can only hope that someday, my children will stand in this spot and think as highly of me and what I've done with my life. JD gave me something to aspire to, something to try to measure up against and something I'll never forget. A sense of family. All of you, all of Compton Pass, are a part of that extended tree. JD told me once that we have so many different jobs to do here that we need all sorts of people. Even ones we don't understand. I think maybe he was trying to tell me something personal then."

He glanced over his shoulder to where Colby and Lucy embraced.

"As the new head of Compass ranch, I plan to uphold his traditions. I was the luckiest bastard in the world to have JD Compton for my father. I'll do my best to be half as decent as him."

Seth was next. He took a step forward. "I could always count on my dad for the truth and a laugh. I don't think I ever realized how much those two things meant to me until the night before my wedding. JD came into the guest room to talk to me since Jody had kicked me out, claiming bad luck." Seth looked at Jody and winked. "He sat down in the chair by the window and he said, 'Son, never start an argument with your wife unless you're right.' I nodded as I always did, appreciating my father's wisdom. I thought about what he'd said and knew that was pretty good advice. I told him I'd keep that in mind. Then JD added, 'And just so you know, you're never gonna be right.'" The crowd laughed. Seth smiled, though there were tear tracks on his cheeks. "My wedding only took place about a month ago, so I haven't had much time to try out his advice, but I'll let you know if JD was speaking the truth. I sort of suspect he is."

Seth stepped back and Vicky wrapped her arm around his

waist. "I can tell you right now, he is."

Leah giggled. There was nothing better than laughter through tears. The beauty of this family was their resilience. Their loss had been tremendous, but even in the face of their pain, they found a way to smile. JD would definitely have approved.

Sam followed when the chuckles trailed off. "All I'd like to say is that my dad was the richest man I knew. He could have lost everything to some hellacious drought, or most likely by giving his last dollar to help someone else, and he'd still have been wealthy. Because he knew that what pays off most is love. I count myself fortunate beyond measure. I won the lotto big-time when it comes to that. And though my gorgeous new wife has also lost a father, we will carry on—live, laugh and thrive—because we have the only thing of any value. My dad showed me every day what it's like to dedicate your soul to a woman and I plan to do just that in his honor."

Sawyer was the last to speak and the pain on his face tore Leah to pieces. "JD told me if you start a journey looking back, maybe you aren't heading in the right direction. When I left for the Coast Guard, I was pretty sure my navigational beacon wasn't pointing due north, but west. I took off, ready to take on the world, a cocky eighteen-year-old. These last few weeks, I've come to realize there isn't one right or wrong direction. A friend reminded me that the point of life isn't to worry about staying the course, it' simply to walk, to put one foot in front of the other."

Sawyer glanced at her and smiled. His face became blurry as her eyes filled.

"It was JD who taught me to walk. He put me on my unsteady feet and let go of my hands. He gave me a taste of the freedom that comes from putting one foot in front of the other and the courage to forge my own path. It was the greatest gift I ever received."

Leah wiped her eyes, the tears flowing rapidly, when Sawyer's voice broke.

Sawyer took a moment to compose himself, then looked out into the crowd. "I thought I'd share his last words to me with all of you because they are simple and true. Be happy. Find what makes you smile and hold on tight to it."

Sawyer returned to his brothers' sides, clasping his mother's hand. Colby invited everyone to return to the house for some dinner. He said, "JD left very few instructions. The one thing he insisted on was, and I quote, 'a big-ass party'."

Everyone laughed as Colby continued. "Nobody loved a barn dance more than JD, and we thought it would be a suitable tribute to him."

The crowd began to disperse, everyone heading to the barn. Leah packed up her guitar and approached Sawyer.

"You hanging in there?"

He nodded. "Yeah. Helps having you here. That song was beautiful, Leah. Thank you." He stroked her cheek lovingly and gave her a sad smile.

They started to return to the house when they noticed Vicky still standing by the grave. Sawyer squeezed her hand.

"Go get her," Leah whispered.

Sawyer went to his mother. He whispered something that made her smile. Sawyer put his arm around Vicky, and he led her slowly toward home.

"It was a wonderful service," Vicky said as they reached the spot where Leah waited for them.

"It really was," Leah agreed.

Vicky looked up at the blue sky and took a deep breath of

the cool autumn air. "We're all going to be fine."

It was a simple statement, but Leah felt the rightness of it.

They would be.

After a huge covered-dish dinner, all the men in attendance started breaking down tables and moving the chairs against the wall of the barn. During the meal, Vicky had recalled the barn dance where she'd first met JD. She'd told everyone in hearing distance about how he'd been the life of the party, leading off the dancing. According to his mother, when it came to community socials, JD was always the first to hit the floor and the last to leave it.

She'd asked Lucy to grab a photo from the family album. Lucy came back with it and they all passed it around laughing. Sawyer had never seen the picture before, but he grinned when he saw the much-younger image of his father. JD was leading a conga line of costumed partiers at a Halloween celebration. His arms were raised, and his smile was contagious.

On the return trip to the house, Sawyer had dreaded the coming evening. Given the heavy emotions of the funeral and the past two days, all he'd wanted to do was go upstairs, crawl into bed and sleep for the next week. However, as always, JD had known the right answer.

Vicky had more color in her face tonight than she'd had in weeks. She was chatting with her friends, eating, reminiscing. Lucy made sure his mother's wineglass was always full and while she was far from drunk, Vicky was certainly relaxed, almost at peace.

The music kicked on, but the floor remained empty. Everyone looked around as if uncertain what to do. Silas caught Sawyer's gaze and nodded. The two of them walked toward the middle of the barn. Sawyer wasn't surprised when Sam and

Seth joined them. The crowd of partygoers laughed as the four brothers started shuffling around and singing along with the music. *Show Me the Way to Go Home* had been JD's favorite song ever since the movie *Jaws* came out. Sawyer couldn't count the number of times he'd heard his dad humming the tune as he worked on the ranch.

Halfway through the song, Seth dragged Vicky out on the floor with them, spinning her around as she laughed. The music continued and soon the barn floor was packed with dancers.

Hours passed, but no one left. No one wanted to break the spell of the magical night. After the heavy emotions of the past month, Sawyer hadn't expected to have so much fun for a very long time.

"Hiya, gorgeous," Leah said. "Where have you been hiding my whole life?"

He caught the distinct smell of tequila on her breath. "Guess I don't have to ask where you gals snuck off to. Enjoy your shots?"

She giggled. Sawyer grinned. He'd never seen Leah tipsy. Just when he thought she couldn't get any cuter, she found a way to surprise him.

"I only had one shot, but wow, my head's sort of spinning."

He wrapped his arm around her shoulder. "Yeah, but you also had a couple glasses of wine with dinner."

"Crap. I forgot about that."

He led her to the door of the barn. "How about some fresh air? Might clear your head."

"Okay." She accepted his proffered hand, and together they meandered away from the party, toward the woods. "I think that's the best dance I've ever been to."

Sawyer agreed. The party ranked up there. "It's been a great night." He sighed and rubbed his hand over his face.

"What's wrong?" Leah asked.

"I'm trying to figure out if I'm supposed to feel this good. I mean, we buried my father this morning. Is this right?"

Leah glanced up at the sky, the moonlight reflected on her face. "I keep thinking about what JD wanted for the family. I remember his last words to you. He said be happy. In a lot of ways, you and your brothers were lucky. You had weeks to say goodbye to your dad, to tell him all the things you wanted to say. There was closure. A lot of people don't get that."

Sawyer nodded. "Never looked at it that way. You're right."

"But more than the closure, you had time to prepare for this. You knew today was coming."

"Yeah. I did."

"And was it as bad as you imagined?"

Sawyer shook his head.

"Nope. Most of the time the things we fear are never as horrible as we imagine. JD only made two requests for his funeral—the moonshine jar and the barn dance. He knew how to live life to the fullest. He suspected his death would be very hard for you, so he found a way to make it easier, to remind you to laugh. If I've learned one thing today, it's that life goes on."

"I love you, Leah."

She smiled. "I never get tired of hearing that."

"Good. Because I intend to say it to you every day for the rest of your life."

Leah laughed. "Careful, cowboy. That sounds perilously close to a proposal."

Sawyer dropped to his knee. "I practiced it a little different, but you're right. That's exactly what it is. Marry me, rose."

203

Leah gasped when he reached into his pocket and pulled out a ring. "Took Mom into town with me last week to help me choose one. We had to get it sized. Marco, the jeweler, tugged me aside and handed it to me tonight."

"You bought me a ring?"

"Why do you sound so surprised?"

She shrugged. "No one can feel this happy. It can't be natural."

Sawyer's grinned widened. "Does that mean you'll marry me?"

Her eyes twinkled with mischief. "Are you giving me a choice? A *real* choice?"

He stood. "Of course I am. So long as you choose right."

"And if I don't?" she teased.

"I'm going to pull a Seth Compton and kidnap you. Tie you to my bed and make love to you until you agree to marry me."

Leah laughed. "God, Saw. You're making this a very hard decision."

Sawyer wrapped his arms around her waist. "What if I promise to tie you up even if you say yes?"

She nodded. "That helps."

She fell silent. Sawyer realized she was having a lot of fun at his expense. "Put me out of my misery, Leah. Yes or no?"

Leah lifted her face to his and kissed him softly. "Yes," she whispered.

"Hot damn. Wait here."

"What?" she asked him, but by that time, Sawyer was ten feet away from her.

"Don't move," he hollered over his shoulder.

"What about my ring?" she yelled.

Sawyer chuckled. He'd been so damned excited by her answer, he'd forgotten to give her the diamond. He rushed back to the barn and searched the crowd until he found who he was looking for.

"Sam." He approached his brother, who was sitting at the edge of the floor, hanging out with several of the hands.

"What's up, bro?"

"Can you and Cindi stay at the ranch house tonight?"

Sam shrugged. "I suppose so. Why?"

"I want to borrow your place."

Sam grinned. "What for?"

Sawyer tilted his head. "You know what for. I've had too much to drink to drive Leah to town. Besides, I'm not sure I could wait that long. She said yes."

"To what?"

"To me. We're getting married."

Sam stood, grabbing Sawyer's hand and shaking it hard. "Well, how about that? The place is all yours. The key to the front door is under the flowerpot at the top of the porch stairs."

Seth and Silas came over.

"What's going on?" Seth asked.

"Sawyer proposed to Leah. She said yes."

Sawyer accepted his brothers' congratulations, their loud cheering bringing their wives and his mother over. After twenty hugs and at least two-dozen congratulatory handshakes, he finally managed to break free. Jesus. Leah was probably thinking he'd deserted her.

He returned to the edge of the woods to find her sitting on the low wall. She gave him an exasperated look. "Thought maybe you'd come to your senses and run away."

He shook his head. "My family."

It was the only explanation he offered, but she didn't seem to need more. "Did they approve?"

"They're over the moon."

"Sawyer?"

He offered her a hand to help her stand. "Yeah?"

"I want my damn ring."

He laughed and placed the diamond on her finger. "We're spending the night at Sam and Cindi's place. They're going to stay at the ranch house."

"Really? Is this part of the tying me to the bed promise?"

"Come on. Let's go consummate this thing."

She laughed. "Do you consummate engagements? Thought that was only marriages."

He grasped her hand and led her down the path that would take them to Sam's cabin. "Leah?"

"Yeah?"

"Walk faster."

Leah giggled, but she let him tug her toward Sam and Cindi's cabin. They ended up racing the last quarter of a mile, both of them breathless by the time they reached the porch.

Sawyer found the key, turned it in the lock and gestured for her to enter. His heart was racing, but not because of the run. It was a new beginning for him tonight. Leah walked into the house. Sawyer paused and glanced toward the clear night sky. He could almost imagine JD smiling down at them.

"You were right, Pa," he whispered. "Like a brick to the face."

"Sawyer?" Leah called from the house.

"Coming, rose."

About the Author

Jayne Rylon and Mari Carr met at a writing conference in June 2009 and instantly became archenemies. Two authors couldn't be more opposite. Mari, when free of her librarian-by-day alter ego, enjoys a drink or two or...more. Jayne, allergic to alcohol, lost huge sections of her financial-analyst mind to an epic explosion resulting from Mari gloating about her hatred of math. To top it off, they both had works in progress with similar titles and their heroes shared a name. One of them would have to go.

The battle between them for dominance was a bloody, but short one, when they realized they'd be better off combining their forces for good (or smut). With the ink dry on the peace treaty, they emerged as good friends, who have a remarkable amount in common despite their differences, and their writing partnership has flourished. Except for the time Mari attempted to poison Jayne with a bottle of Patron. Accident or retaliation? You decide.

Jayne and Mari can be found troublemaking on their Yahoo loop at: http://groups.yahoo.com/group/Heat_Wave_Readers.

You can follow their book-loving insanity on Twitter or Facebook or send them a personal note at contact@jaynerylon.com or carmichm1@yahoo.com.

It's all about the story...

Romance

HORROR

www.samhainpublishing.com

CPSIA information can be obtained at www.ICGtesting.com
Printed in the USA
LVOW081618190113

316415LV00004B/29/P